6堂課學會英文速讀

6
堂課
學會
英文速讀

周昱翔——著

目次

英文速讀

A Primer on Speed Reading
with Greater Comprehension

為什麼要讀這本書？

　　過去40年來，老師教閱讀的方式就是查單字、記文法，一篇閱讀至少要讀十分鐘以上，換句話說，學習閱讀的方式就是不斷地查單字，並且背許多文法規則。而考試時，由於必須仰賴解題技巧，學生常常被訓練成填鴨式考試機器，考前衝刺，考完就還給老師。

　　在台灣學生所面對的各項英文考試中（從國中會考、大學學測、指考、多益，到留學考試托福、雅思等），閱讀能力總是扮演決定性角色，然而閱讀測驗卻是讓台灣學生最頭痛的部分之一。關鍵原因是考試時間有限，考生必須在有限時間內，看完而且看懂多篇文章，所以常常耗費很多時間去理解文章到底是什麼意思，終於看完文章之後，卻往往沒有足夠的時間仔細檢查每個選項中的陷阱。在英文考試中，花費過多時間閱讀文章無疑讓考生處於劣勢。唯有更有效率地正確理解文意才能夠在考試中取得優勢。因此「若我能夠閱讀再快一點的話就好了」，可以說是台灣學生在英文學習路上的共同心聲！

　　為何考試要限時間呢？這是因為出題者需要鑑別學生的程度，程度較好的學生有能力在比較短的時間內讀懂文章，然後正確回答題目，閱讀看不完的考生自然顯示其較差之語言程度，也就是說，考試壓縮時間的目的就是要鑑別考生的英文程度。即便考生有能力看懂文章，但若無法在考試時間內閱讀完所有文章，便無法回答完考題，無法取得高分。因此閱讀速度可以說是各項英文考試高分的潛規則！近年來，國內外的英文考試有兩個主流趨勢：①對單字量的要求減少，②閱讀量增加，考試時間卻不增加。這兩個趨勢就是為了要加強檢驗學生的閱讀效率，而非死背的單字多寡。

　　舉例來說，108年教育部新課綱大量減少高中單字量，從7000字下修，要求學生學習英文不要只背單字，因此減少艱深晦澀的字彙，聚焦大考常見的4500字。因應國際化的教育方針，新課綱要求的「核心素養」即為學生真實的「理解力」，並非粗淺的認識單字就好。1926年就開始實施的美國的大學入學考試SAT也是如此，2016年推出的新制SAT大幅下降單字難度，因為美國大考中心認為學生只認識單字並不等於具備讀懂文章的能力，所以SAT的設計使考生必須真正讀懂文章，充分理解文意後才能夠答對題目。不論是國內的學測、指考，或是國外的SAT，都已無法全用關鍵字的技巧，閃避閱讀全文直接解題，這對於閱讀速度慢的同學而言，無疑是很大的挑戰。

另外一個趨勢就是閱讀量增加，考試時間卻不增加。一個明顯的例子即為多益，多益在台灣常被當作是英語能力的指標之一，但2018年推出新制多益的字彙難度沒有太多改變，但是閱讀篇數卻明顯增多，而考試時間沒有隨之增加。如此壓縮時間的目的就是要加強考驗閱讀速度。因此考生普遍抱怨時間不夠題目根本答不完！即便考生有能力看懂文章，卻常常無法在考試時間內閱讀完所有文章，故難以取得高分。

美國另一種大學入學考試ACT對考生的閱讀能力都有嚴格的考察。ACT嚴格要求閱讀速度，只有35分鐘要回答40題，而新制SAT更直接取消短篇閱讀，全部改為長篇閱讀。兩種入學考試皆加強檢驗學生能在有限時間內讀完文章，並且展現較高的理解力。

許多台灣學生計畫出國留學時，常常托福與雅思考了好多次，文章還是看不完，這是因為托福與雅思的長篇閱讀相較於其他測驗來得更長，考生作答長篇閱讀時，緊迫的時間便是最大的問題。近年來托福、雅思文章的長度與難度皆有增加，越來越接近GRE與GMAT（美國研究所入學考試）的程度，若無法突破托福與雅思的長篇閱讀，將很難獲得高分，不易被國外名校錄取。

舉凡各項英文考試，考察考生的閱讀力為共同趨勢，各種英文考試的閱讀普遍加長、篇數增加，時間卻沒有增加，以壓縮時間的方式加強考驗考生的閱讀效率。即便考生有能力看懂文章，但若無法在時間內閱讀完所有文章，便無法完成作答，與高分失之交臂。

　　本書提出的「高理解英文速讀」是更有效率的閱讀方式，傳聞美國總統羅斯福與甘迺迪都具備英文速讀的能力，能夠高效率閱讀完每日堆積如山的公文。據說羅斯福總統每天吃早餐的時間就可以看完一本書；紐約時報更曾報導過，畢業於哈佛大學的甘迺迪總統閱讀速度驚人，並且重視英文速讀，在他擔任美國總統期間，要求白宮員工必須要學英文速讀，才能更有效率地為人民服務。

　　本書主要目的係協助台灣學生增強英文閱讀的能力，進而達到高理解英文速讀的目標。讓台灣學生能夠具備更強的閱讀實力，在各種考試中（學測、指考、多益、托福、雅思、SAT/ACT、GRE/GMAT等）取得高分。本書為入門自學書籍，是把英文變簡單的方式，能夠讓學生更容易看懂英文閱讀。按照書中的教學與練習即可感受到「高理解」英文速讀的力量，本書共有六堂課程，能夠幫助學生領悟高理解英文速讀的方法，並作為自己閱讀練習的準則。在準備考試時，不再只是仰賴投機性質的解題技巧。第五堂課與第六堂課也特別提供多篇高理解英文速讀的練習（本書選用大學學測與指考的閱讀試題作為練習），幫助學生快速理解英文閱讀，並檢測自己的閱讀理解力。

　　最後要強調的是，學好英文沒有捷徑，「英文速讀」不是「英文速成」，並不是一蹴可幾，但是好的方法可以讓我們事半功倍。我相信「高理解英文速讀」就像任何其他學校科目一樣，至少需要一段時間有系統性的學習與引導練習，才能夠在英文理解速度上有所提升，在考試中更勝一籌。

推薦序一

《6 堂課學會英文速讀》──學術實用的利劍

張淑英

（前台大國際長、西班牙皇家學院外籍院士）

西班牙文常用 "Cada maestrillo tiene su librillo"（各師各法）這個俚語用在教育、教學上，為教師正名/證明，表示為人師表各有一套、各顯神通的妙方。而教學，之所以為師，常常援引學術方法論來「各施各法」。但是，師/施之法最重要的是讓接收的學習者能懂，會用，知變，暢通。

周昱翔教授這本《6 堂課學會英文速讀》言簡意賅，先點出了五種認知錯誤的英文速讀迷思，並且解析三種中英文在文化、邏輯和文法上的差異，學理開門見山，釋疑更一針見血。我們長期以來一直探討台灣的英語教育和考試效能，尤其大學前最強調的閱讀能力，常有處處彌補卻又處處漏洞的質疑，《6 堂課學會英文速讀》以學術的專業和實務的操作提供正確的策略，不僅僅是考試的閱讀有方，更是「讀之有物」的思辨理解。

《6 堂課學會英文速讀》以97–107 十年來指考或學測的英文試題為解析素材以便更貼近讀者。近年來英文試題的趨勢為篇幅長但不艱澀，以短時間挑戰有效且正確的理解為導向。這表示英文教與學要以日常生活英文化為標的，從考試中得到育/寓、教、樂的啟示，因此英文的學習、測驗、訓練、應用是結合常識、知識和智性的涵養。我認為本書所欲強調的英文速讀養成，好比數學的心算訓練，是一套有系統邏輯的思考和籌慮。周昱翔教授極有系統地析透關鍵詞組和構句法，說明把握人、物、動作和時地的閱讀方法，即能達陣致勝。「高理解速讀」的葵花寶典是因為腦中有算盤，手中有數字和次序（包括逆向或倒裝），繼而算出正確答案，達到「有意義」的閱讀。

　　十年前，周昱翔教授在外文系擔任專任講師時我便認識他，常在系上迴廊間錯身，彼此問候或交談，我見他凡事總是全力以赴，精益求精。四年教學期間兩度獲得全校教學優良獎；爾後以教育部、美國國務院、密西根大學的各種獎學金前往密西根大學攻讀博士，四年內即取得博士學位。

　　2017年，他捨棄大華語地區高薪的教職，執意回到故鄉致力教學，回到外文系任教。我見他十年如一日，猶如十年磨一劍，把他在密西根大學的學術專業帶回台灣，致力精進台灣的英語教學，幫助學子的英語學習朝向國際化、英語化的境界。過去五年五個月期間，我剛好擔任台灣大學國際長，我戲謔自己是從「西遊記」（西語學者）到「三國演義」（中文、西文、英文）走國際的跨文化經驗，工作與生活的速度經常追趕跑跳碰，使用英文，閱讀英文更是關鍵，深刻感受到有效率的理解和正確的使用是成事的良方，搭建國際交流的橋樑。如今再閱讀周昱翔教授的《6 堂課學會英文速讀》，更覺得它是化繁為簡，出計攻城的利劍。

2019年1月28日

推薦序二

學好英語的秘密武器

高維泓
（台大外文系教授）

　　台灣的學生在英語學習上最容易碰到的瓶頸之一，就是背了好多單字，但是當一篇完整的文章呈現在眼前，就彷彿陷入十里霧中，好像有看懂，但又不太確定是否正確。為何會造成這種情況，一方面是台灣的英語教育，過度重視「背單字」。固然字彙量太少，的確會造成閱讀障礙，但硬背單字卻不知語意間的「組合關係」，就像在超市買了一堆食材，但不知如何處理，煮出來的不是佳餚，連自己看了都倒胃口。

　　有許多人以為歐洲人似乎學習英語比亞洲人快，一種說法是英語繼承了印歐語系（如法語、日耳曼語、義大利語、拉丁語等）的許多字彙與特點，省卻了不少單字學習上的障礙。這個說法其是有待商榷的。為何許多台灣的大學生從小學英文，學了十數年，用填鴨方式背誦記下無數的字首、字根、同義字、反義字、衍生字等，但一遇到長篇閱讀便只能胡猜一通導致誤讀，考試成績低落，甚至覺得自己沒有語言天份，還是放棄吧！到底我們的英語教育和學習方式出了什麼問題？

　　容我很坦白的告訴大家，英文學的好不好，跟語文天份一點關係也沒有。事實上，「單字填鴨」從來不是歐美教師的教學策略，「大量閱讀」才是他們交給學生的釣竿，是提昇英語能力的關鍵。單字充其量只是食材，大量且廣泛地閱讀才能讓學習者成為一個靈活的釣手。

　　許多人學不好英文的原因跟台灣的英語教育不夠重視「閱讀方法」有關。也就是說，當有一篇陌生的文章在眼前，只能從第一個字開始讀嗎？能否先掌握語意的邏輯，進而理解文章內容？請大家試想，當我們閱讀中文報紙新聞，即使報導很長，事件也很複雜，但依舊能夠有很高的理解能力。為何可以如此？正是因為我們對於中文語意產生的方式已經有所掌握（甚至早已建置於腦海裡）。換言之，眼睛所看到的字詞其實是搭配中文的語意結構填骨架肉上去的。如果認得很多中文字詞，卻不識得文章前後的邏輯關聯，即便識得康熙字典裡所有晦澀艱深的字詞，也都只是徒勞。

周昱翔博士的這本《6堂課學會英文速讀》就是一本讓英語學習者突破盲點的英語學習教材。在這個知識與資訊爆炸的全球化時代，如能加快英文閱讀能力，必然能比其他人更快掌握機會。就讓教學經驗豐富的周博士一步步為你指點迷津吧！

2019年2月25日

Empowering Students

As is often the case, many students in Taiwan spend much time memorizing vocabulary and grammatical rules, and yet they do not read well enough or quickly enough to ensure comprehension. It is a problem that has been hiding in plain sight for decades. When Taiwanese students were measured against international benchmarks, they were often not on par with their counterparts in neighboring countries. This should be a wake-up call. It seems obvious that English education in Taiwan has been stuck in neutral for years, students' reading efficiency being a case in point. Reading at a satisfactory rate remains a major challenge for most students in Taiwan. This is particularly evident when they read within the limited time frame on a test. Quite simply put, they read way too slow and should not settle for less.

Picking up speed alone, however, will not lead to better comprehension. It is the other way around. Comprehension comes before speed and greater comprehension depends on an ability to identify meaningful units of text. It is in this light that this book adopts a meaning-based approach to connecting language forms with meaning in contexts of use, a radical departure from the traditional form-focused pedagogy. This book demonstrates how new skills come into play in the act of reading. Readers will walk away with increased attention to meaning-making in texts and a deeper understanding of how texts unfold in written genres.

Y.S.J.

Ph.D., University of Michigan, Ann Arbor

第一堂課

英文速讀的 NG 觀念

這堂課要討論的英文速讀 NG 觀念包括：

常見的 9 種閱讀方式

NG觀念❶ 速讀就是一知半解的「略讀」，只是走馬看花

NG觀念❷ 速讀就是迅速翻頁和擴大視野的技巧

NG觀念❸ 只要背單字記文法，考試就一定可以看得懂

NG觀念❹ 大量閱讀與速度沒什麼關係

NG觀念❺ 右腦圖像記憶法可以讓我們看得更快

常見的 9 種英文閱讀方式

首先，我們需要知道「英文閱讀」其實有很多種類，常見的 9 種英文閱讀方式為：

❶正常閱讀 reading

❷高理解速讀 reading with greater comprehension and speed

❸廣泛閱讀 extensive reading

❹窄式閱讀 narrow reading

❺略讀 skimming

❻掃讀 scanning

❼特定區域細讀 close reading

❽密集反覆式閱讀 intensive reading

❾思辨式閱讀 critical / analytical reading

首先，「正常閱讀」reading 的意思是看完全部的文章並且充分理解文章意思。而「高理解速讀」reading with greater comprehension and speed 就是花費較少的時間，看完全部的文章並且充分理解文章內容，高理解速讀即為快速閱讀的意思，所以尤其適合時間緊迫的各項考試。

我們常常聽到要增加閱讀量，才能夠增強英語能力，培養出這個常聽到的抽象詞彙—英文語感，這也就是所謂的「廣泛閱讀」extensive reading 的目標。「廣泛閱讀」就是透過閱讀不同的文體和主題，廣泛涉獵多元知識，包含文學、人文社會、經濟文化、自然科學、商業科技、歷史地理、藝術娛樂、節能環保、體育運動等，藉此拓展學生的知識廣度和深度，因而培養語感，像母語人士般自然的理解英文。問題是，沒有一定的閱讀速度，廣泛閱讀幾乎不可能做到。台灣學生的閱讀速度普遍較慢，看完一篇文章常花上十分鐘，因此「廣泛閱讀」雖為學校老師念茲在茲的期待，卻少有人能夠真正做到，其核心原因便是缺乏速度，這也就是英文速讀重要的原因。英文速讀不只能幫助學生在考場占盡時間優勢，更能讓學生在平日以較少的時間閱讀更多的英文，進而培養英文實力，畢竟台灣學生很忙碌，要讀的科目很多，時間卻有限。

「窄式閱讀」 narrow reading 則是指閱讀類似主題或相同作者的文章，目的是讓學生比較容易注意到反覆出現的單字或文法句型，是學習單字和文法的方式之一，但是「窄式閱讀」主要的目標並不是提升閱讀速度。

另外一種閱讀方式為「略讀」skimming，這是一種省略內容的閱讀方式，只有閱讀部分的文章內容而已。略讀多是瀏覽各段的第一句，希望以較少的時間對文章能夠略知一二，這種閱讀的方式能夠粗略了解文章結構與大綱，但僅是一知半解，對文章的整體理解度偏低。

還有一種只需要少量時間便可完成的閱讀方式，這種方式稱為「掃讀」scanning，掃讀就像是在掃描文章一樣，在文章中搜尋特定的字詞，就像是在電話簿中搜尋某人的電話號碼一樣，其他內容完全不看，因為掃讀只有一個目的，就是搜尋特定的人名、時間、地點，或相關詞語，因此對文章整體的理解度較低。

另一種閱讀方式為「特定區域細讀」close reading，這種閱讀方式即為逐字看文章中特定的部分，例如合約中特別重要的部分，但並不看完整篇文章，這種閱讀方式的速度較緩慢，但是理解力高。

台灣傳統的英文教學方式則是「密集反覆式閱讀」 intensive reading，這種閱讀方式的目標不只是理解文章內容，更包含了學習文章中的單字和文法，也就是學生需要逐字逐句查出不認識的單字，了解每個不認識單字的意思、詞性，以及用法。在台灣的英文課堂中，包含了學習相關的字根、字首、同義字、反義字，以及衍生字，同時需要學習每條不懂的文法規則。單單一篇文章就需要花費許多時間，優點是學生能夠充分看懂文章內容，缺點是即便是一篇短文章就需要耗時10分鐘以上。

最後一種閱讀方式為大學生或研究生在閱讀長達數十頁的學術性論文時，常常需要使用的「思辨式閱讀」critical/ analytical reading。這種閱讀方式的主要目標是提供思考各種問題的機會，培養學生的思辨能力，能夠面對沒有明確答案的問題。也就是說,對所閱讀的文章進行思辨,檢視邏輯的合理性,分析證據,論證並評估優劣,最後做出判斷,得到客觀的結論。在高等教育的學術研究裡,「思辨式閱讀」是教授、研究生、研究人員每日做研究的必要工具。他們需要仔細客觀的思考所閱讀的內容,反覆地閱讀並仔細作筆記,仔細檢視作者每個論點是否合理,作者所提出的證據是否夠充分並讓其論點更站得住腳;同時,為了評估文章的研究方法是否嚴謹,需要閱讀其他相關文獻,做許多延伸閱讀,以至於能夠明確指出文章之長處與缺失。在學術期刊的評審工作中,評審需要判斷文章內容是否對這個領域有創新的價值,並向期刊主編建議是否接受、拒絕,或要求修改該篇研究論文。

英文閱讀的方式和定義

閱讀方式	定義
正常閱讀 （reading）	看完全文並且充分理解文意。
高理解速讀 （reading with greater comprehension and speed）	用較短的時間,看完全文並且充分理解文意,適合時間有限的考試。
廣泛閱讀 （extensive reading）	大量閱讀多樣化題材的文章,閱讀速度緩慢者很難做到,因為如果速度慢,大量閱讀將會耗費相當長的時間。
窄式閱讀 （narrow reading）	閱讀類似主題或相同作者的文章,因此學生比較容易注意到反覆出現的詞彙與文法句型。是學習單字和文法結構的方式之一。
略讀 （skimming）	只用少量的時間,綜覽各段第一句,粗略了解文章結構,但對全文理解力低,容易一知半解。

掃讀 （scanning）	在文章中搜尋特定的字詞 (就如同在電話簿中搜尋某人的號碼)，其他內容完全不看，對全文理解度低。
特定區域細讀 （close reading）	逐字看文章中特定的部分，但不看完整篇文章。
密集反覆式閱讀 （intensive reading）	逐字逐句查出生字和學習文法規則，同一篇文章密集反覆閱讀許多次，一篇短文章就需耗時10分鐘以上。
思辨式閱讀 （critical/ analytical reading）	通常指閱讀長達數十頁的學術性論文，緩慢地閱讀並作筆記，仔細檢視論點是否合理，證據是否充分，同時需要閱讀相關文獻，評估文章研究方法是否嚴謹，是否對這個領域有創新價值，並指出文章內容的長處與缺失。

　　在了解英文閱讀的幾種方式之後，接下來我們來討論一下常見的NG觀念：

NG觀念 ❶

速讀就是一知半解的「略讀」，只是走馬看花

　　世界知名的英國劍橋字典（Cambridge Dictionary）定義閱讀為 "to look at words and understand what they mean"。美國權威韋氏字典（Merriam-Webster's Dictionary）定義閱讀為 "to look at and understand the meaning of letters, words, symbols, etc"。由這兩本國際主要英語字典明確的定義可知，閱讀二字包含了「閱」──看或看見，和「讀」──理解所看見文字的意思。閱讀二字表示不只是看見文字，更包含理解文字的意思。

　　速讀二字有「快速」與「閱讀」兩個層面的意思，與「閱讀」唯一的差別就是速度。換言之，速讀是擁有正常水準的「理解力」，但是只需要較少的時間便可以讀完整篇文章。倘若只有快速看過去而無法充分理解文意，充其量只能稱為「速閱」而不能稱為「速讀」，因為速讀的正確定義為「具備理解力的快速閱讀」。

　　在此要特別強調「有效」effective 和「效率」efficient 這兩字在閱讀上不同的意思，當我們花了10分鐘閱讀一篇文章，充分理解文章的意思，這稱為「有效閱讀」effective reading，但是並沒有「效率」 efficient，因為耗費了10分鐘的時間；如果只用了2分鐘閱讀完原本需要10分鐘的文章，而且獲得一樣理解力，這則稱作「效率」efficient。因此速讀不只是 effective reading，更是 efficient reading。

　　常常有人誤解「略讀」（skimming）就等於是「速讀」，其實這是不正確的，因為速讀的前提是對所閱讀的文章具有高度的理解力，而「略讀」並不具備高理解力。因為「略讀」意為省略閱讀某些內容，只看主題句（topic sentence）或每段起始處或各段的第一句/首句，尋找文中的關鍵字，粗略了解文章主旨，因為並沒有閱讀大部分的內容，所以對全文理解力偏低，因為理解力低，感覺上有如走馬看花，容易一知半解。任何號稱一分鐘可以看1000-2000 英文字的閱讀方法其實都只是「略讀」。本書討論的是具備高度理解力的「高理解英文速讀」，強調理解力必須優先於速度的追求。

NG觀念❷

速讀就是迅速翻頁和擴大視野的技巧

　　閱讀速度慢的人通常視野廣度較小，每次只能夠注視一個字，單單一個句子就必須看好多次，由於一個字一個字逐字讀的速度常常連我們大腦思考的速度都趕不上，因此容易讓人走神分心，如果一不小心閃神，又得從頭再看一次，白白浪費了許多時間。如果能夠訓練眼球移動速度，尤其是視線移動的技巧，加上用手指做引導成波浪型或X字形或Z字形軌跡，便可以讓我們眼睛移動更快一點，甚至能夠「一目十行」。所謂一目十行即是將多行文字形成一個畫面的方式 (像是看風景圖片那樣)。不是以「點」的方式，而是以「面」的方式看文章，就如同我們看照片或圖像那樣，一眼就可以看一行以上，甚至一眼就能看完一整頁。因此能夠迅速翻頁。

　　但是事實上，認知科學的研究發現，當我們眼睛看得越快，理解力通常會變得越差。所以強調視線移動的技巧並無法提升閱讀理解力。由於人類的閱讀視野是有限的，眼睛的生理構造所允許的「有效視角」也是有限的，過度寬闊的閱讀視野無助於理解力，而且眼球移動速度太快，視線將會變得模糊，因此，不論是強調眼睛移動技巧，或是手指移動巧思，其目的都只是針對速度的增加，而不是為了提升閱讀理解力。任何聲稱能夠「一目十行」的閱讀方式，很可能只會有「一知半解」的結果，有如走馬看花般不扎實，對於閱讀理解力亦無太多助益。

　　閱讀的首要目的應該是了解文章意思，在這個前提下，提升速度才是有意義的。如果沒有看懂文章，眼球或手指移動再快速仍舊無助於瞭解文章的意思。換言之，為了追求速度而（暫時）犧牲理解力的方式是錯誤的，並不會因為閱讀速度變快就魔術般的全部理解了，反倒會因為速度走在理解力前面，而讓理解力難以提升。

　　如果像訓練飛行員那樣，用儀器或電腦螢幕，用幾分之一秒的時間閃過一個字，只為了訓練學生用最短時間去分辨一個字，追求表面的速度，但是卻完全忽略英文的meaning，這樣的視線訓練並無法提升理解力。畢竟一篇英文文章是由許多有意義的群組（meaningful units）組成並產生有意義的訊息，因此「高理解英文速讀」並不是一次看一整句，或一次看整個段落，更不是一次看整頁那樣的華而不實。「高理解英文速讀」重視能夠多快速地「理解」所見文字，而不是能夠多快速地「看見」這些文字。

「高理解英文速讀」是改變看英文的方式，強調的是更清晰的視線，獲得更高的理解力，以及前兩者所產生更快的速度（並非一味追求速度而已）。「高理解英文速讀」能讓學生立即感受到理解力的提升，進而只需要較少的時間便可以充分理解文意，如此速度的增加才是有意義的。

NG觀念❸

只要背單字記文法，考試就一定可以看得懂

明明單字都認識，文法規則也背的超熟，考試時，閱讀還是看很慢！而且常常同一句反覆看許多遍，看下一句就忘了上一句在說甚麼，因此常常耗費許多時間。

這是因為閱讀不是在考單字文法，並不是單字量夠多，就一定能在考試時間內看完且看懂閱讀文章。為什麼考試閱讀這麼長，給考生的時間卻又這麼短？最主要的目的就是要鑑別考生不同的英文程度，因為只有語言能力較好的學生，才有能力在考試時間內讀完看懂文章，並有足夠時間仔細審題，答對題目。如果閱讀的速度夠快，自然能有更多時間去找出答題所需的資訊。因此閱讀看不完的考生自然顯示其程度較差，閱讀速度可說是各項英文考試高分的潛規則。

在英文閱讀測驗中，學生需要在看懂文章之後，於測驗題目中選出正確的答案。考試中耗費時間的除了閱讀文章本身，還有找出每題答案的時間。因此，學生在閱讀文章上面花費越多的時間，能夠仔細審題的時間就越少。畢竟，學生在閱讀測驗中的最終目標是答對測驗的題目，花費再多的時間閱讀文章不等於能夠答對陷阱重重的題目。

過去台灣的英文教育方式，教閱讀其實就是在教單字教文法，並沒有讓

學生學習有效閱讀的方式，由於大部分的台灣學生閱讀速度偏慢，考試緊張速度只會更慢，因此答題時間直接被壓縮，所以，許多英文老師會鼓勵學生仰賴解題技巧，考試前，老師的任務就是歸類各種題目類型，希望學生能夠仰賴解題技巧（而非本身的閱讀實力），取得高分，常見的解題技巧包含：

①直接先看題目，看題目之後再回頭去看文章找題目中的「關鍵字」，一個訓練有素的考生能夠在題目中快速找到「關鍵字」，比如說人名、日期等，為了省下一些時間，只使用「掃讀」的方式，搜尋文章中的關鍵字，希望仰賴關鍵字的捷徑，能夠片面了解文意，省時間又不需要閱讀全文。而且答案選項常常就直接一字不漏地出現在文章裡面。

的確，過去有些時候的確可以從文章中斷章取義，只根據原文某個片段來作答，所以有些老師會要求學生跳過文章，直接從題目找關鍵字。但是，靠關鍵字直接答對的題目其實是屬於低階考題，語言測驗的研究證實缺乏鑑別度，尤其在早期英文考試，出題水準不如現在，信度和效度都不如現今的考題，現在的英文考試已無法全用關鍵字的答題技巧直接解題，必須讀懂文章，越來越多高階考題都必須要看完全文才有可能看懂題目的問題核心，更加要求學生要充分理解文意後才有能力正確答題，如果對全文和其他內容的關聯性不清楚，只靠題目的關鍵字反而容易讓學生誤解文意，掉入考題的陷阱。

②千萬不要讀完整篇文章，只採取「略讀」的方式，也就是說，只閱讀每一段的前兩句，或段落主題句，然後就直接解題，希望以表淺的理解力就可以拿到理想分數。

過去 40 年來，台灣不乏仰賴這些解題技巧而獲得高分的「解題機器」，

由於這些高分並不是考生的閱讀實力，學生考完試常會有心虛的感覺，因為考試完，只留下了解題技巧，閱讀實力仍是原地踏步，學生有沒有實力，自己心裡最清楚，這也就是為什麼台灣有許多學生明明獲得了高分，卻對自己英文程度沒有信心。只用解題技巧獲得的分數通常缺乏高分背後所代表的英文程度，導致學生進入國內外大學或職場之後，英文程度不足、學習落後，信心也受到打擊。

尤其，這種「略讀」的方式對文章常常會一知半解，尤其對於現在普遍閱讀加長加多的考試趨勢，從學測的 1400 字左右到 SAT 的 4500 字左右的閱讀量（如下圖所示），就是要檢驗考生是否能在時間壓力下，對所閱讀的文章有足夠的理解，並且能夠留下充分的時間仔細回答題目。因此「略讀」對於考生是弊大於利，尤其文章越長，「略讀」的理解力只會越低，面對陷阱重重的題目時，很容易因為對全文理解不足的緣故，許多選項看起來好像都是對的，因此常常要重新再「略讀」文章一次，如此一來，這種「略讀」的捷徑反而消耗更多時間，造成本末倒置的結果。題目就算全部做完了，也是題題沒有把握。

考試種類	閱讀量
學測	4 篇（每篇約 250-350 字）
指考	4 篇（每篇約 300-400 字）
多益	單篇 10 篇（每篇約 100-300 字） 多篇型文章共 5 組（每組多篇共約 300-900 字）
托福	3–4 篇（每篇約 700-800 字）
雅思	3 篇（每篇約 800-900 字）
SAT	5 篇（每篇約 700-900 字）
ACT	4 篇（每篇約 900 字）

就如同會單字文法不一定能看懂文章一樣的道理，提升閱讀理解力是方法的問題，如果使用錯誤的方式，即便是簡單的文章也無法很快地看完讀

懂。花太多時間閱讀文章，無法仔細看題目，容易掉入題目設計的陷阱中，因此只有「高理解」速讀才能夠讓我們有充分時間答題，避開選項陷阱，獲得高分。

NG觀念❹

大量閱讀與速度沒什麼關係

許多學生都知道要大量閱讀，因為大量閱讀能夠獲得廣博知識，增加考試戰力，英文閱讀實力更為堅強，的確，閱讀量夠大，英文實力會更上層樓。

只是，如果閱讀速度緩慢，如何能夠做到大量閱讀？要耗費多少時間才能夠達到「大量」的目標？如果無法達到一定的閱讀速度，將容易陷入惡性循環（如下圖）。

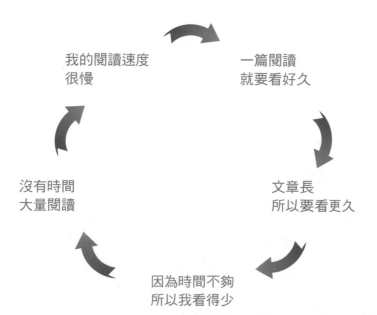

我的閱讀速度
很慢

一篇閱讀
就要看好久

文章長
所以要看更久

因為時間不夠
所以我看得少

沒有時間
大量閱讀

通常來說，閱讀慢的學生光是閱讀一篇文章就要耗費許久的時間，若是遇到長度較長的文章則要花更多的時間，但是平常上課念書繁忙，根本沒有這麼多時間閱讀英文，因此沒有足夠的時間，自然閱讀量相當少，因為閱讀量少的緣故，閱讀速度依舊緩慢，陷入這樣惡性循環的學生在台灣其實很常見。所以說，「高理解英文速讀」是大量閱讀的必要條件，本書所提出的「高理解英文速讀」是把英文變簡單的方式，能夠讓學生更容易看懂文章，有感提升閱讀理解力。

NG觀念❺

右腦圖像記憶法可以讓我們看得更快

右腦圖像記憶通常透過有趣的圖像或動畫增加記憶力，也就是說，可以將閱讀中的文字圖像化，然後記憶這個圖像所代表的訊息。然而，相關研究證明所有語言與文字訊息主要都是由我們的左腦處理的。左腦是理性的，擅於線性的思考，重視步驟順序。對於語言這種符號能夠加以定義、分析、比較、推理和應用。左腦的運作重視邏輯，可以有條理地分門別類我們所接受到的訊息。

然而，我們的右腦是感性的。主要負責處理我們所接觸的圖案以及影像，是靈感與藝術的來源，對於音樂、韻律或圖像等訊息，能夠轉換成不同的感受和想像。右腦圖像的記憶法就是將文字轉換成圖像訊息來理解記憶。

可是將文字圖像化這個過程所需的時間卻是因人而異，對許多人來說並不容易。由於每一個人的想像力不同，對於同一個物件，不同的人所想到的事物與經驗感受也不盡相同。右腦圖像記憶法也許可以讓我們慢慢咀嚼文字本身的意思，在腦中浮現具體的圖像或是抽象的概念。可是每一次轉換的過程通常會需要數秒鐘，甚至幾分鐘的時間才能想像出來一個字的意像是什麼。這是一種記憶的方法，但不容易直接提升閱讀速度。

在考試中，閱讀的時間有限，閱讀測驗的目的並不是測驗考生的記憶力，考生不需要牢牢地把文章內容記住才能夠正確答題，閱讀測驗的目的是測驗考生能夠多快正確地理解文章意思，並找出正確的題目選項。所以正確理解文章是前提，速度快慢則決定分數高低。

我相信唯有能夠快速理解文章的學生，才能夠在考場獲得更充份時間仔細答題。也就是說，別人讀一遍的時間，高理解英文速讀的學生能夠詳讀二到三遍，自然對文章的理解力更高，更有可能答對題目。

第二堂課

英文與中文的語言差異

這堂課要討論英文與中文的差異包括：

- **-1-** 文化的差異
- **-2-** 邏輯的差異
- **-3-** 文法的差異

　　孫子兵法有云：「知己知彼，百戰百勝。」不了解敵人，只了解自己，勝敗的機會各佔一半；不了解敵人，也不了解自己，註定要失敗。學習英文閱讀亦是如此，一個母語是中文的學生想要學好英文，就必須先了解中文這個語言，才能夠充分理解與體會英文的意思。

　　對於台灣學生來說，中文閱讀不需要顧慮語言的問題，對於受過學校基礎教育的台灣學生來說，沒有一句中文是看不懂的（這邊指的是當代白話文，非古代文言文）。然而，英文閱讀完全不同於中文閱讀。不單只是因為英文不是台灣學生的母語，更是因為中文與英文在世界語言的「族譜」上，距離相對較遠，因此，台灣學生學習英文的難度就會比，舉例來說，西班牙學生學習英文來得更困難一些。然而，如果是學習中文的話，日本學生通常會比美國學生更容易上手，這正是因為日語在漢字上借用了許多中文字，拉近了中文和日語這兩種語言的距離。此外，中文與英文這兩種語言有著完全不同的書寫系統，英文是拼音文字，而中文則是表意文字。因此語法結構和語意表達的方式也不盡相同。

　　由於英文不是台灣學生的母語，理解英文文章並不像是母語人士那樣的直接反應。除了字彙量之外，難度更在於學生如何能夠正確理解每個句子的意思。第二語言習得（Second Language Acquisition）的相關研究文獻指出，非母語學習者有著不同的文化背景，不同使用語言的經驗，和不同的語言邏輯。這些都對於理解英文閱讀有一定程度的影響。

　　我與 8 位台大老師於 2012 年合寫的一本教學知能專書中的〈從語言邏輯培養思辨能力〉一章節就指出語言的學習跟語言邏輯有著密不可分的關係。不同的語言，使用的邏輯也是不同的。因為這兩種語言的歷史發展，文化意涵都不一樣，自然他們的語言邏輯也不盡相同。如果希望英文閱讀理解力高，台灣學生必須要對這兩種語言的思考邏輯有一定程度的了解。

　　本書是以英文的 meaning 作為出發點，幫助學生提升對英文語意的理解力。然而 meaning 的詮釋可能會受到許多因素的影響，所以這一課針對文化、思考邏輯、文法等中英差異做為舉例與說明，幫助台灣學生充分了解這些因素對於英文 meaning 的詮釋所可能產生的影響。

❶文化的差異

英文和中文這兩種文字間存在思維差異，而象形或形象的比喻多源自於文化歷史、民俗民情、及社會約定俗成等背景。這也就是為什麼電子翻譯機、電腦翻譯或 Google 翻譯尚未能夠做到精準翻譯的緣故。

在台灣，學生學習英文時最常見的現象就是逐字翻譯自己所看到的每一句英文，常常希望自己能夠一個字一個字將英文直接翻譯成中文，然後以中文的邏輯去理解文意。當然，任何語言都一定多少會有類似甚至可以直接翻譯轉換的字詞，舉例來說：

英文中的 eye-opening 就是中文的大開眼界，形容某件事或事件的發生讓我們很驚訝，因為我們從來沒有聽過，看過，或體驗過類似事情。

另外，a turning point 也就是中文說的轉捩點，用來形容某一個事件對於一個人或事物產生巨大的影響，因而改變其之後的發展。

Get a big head 就是中文常說的「大頭症」，用來形容一個人成功了以後就開始自視甚高，變得比較傲慢。

當我們看到好吃的東西，我們會說，我都流口水了，用來表達食物看起還很美味的意思，英文則可以說 It is making my mouth water.，同樣形容食物感覺很美味，讓我們很想要吃的意思。

但是，並不是每一個中文字都能夠對應到另一個英文字，反之亦然，這是因為不同的語言有不同的文化背景，這些文化因素常常會影響我們該如何正確理解英文的意思，舉例來說，中文的「回籠覺」就沒有相對應的英文字，那美國人有沒有睡回籠覺呢？有，但是他們沒有一個專門的字，所以當他們睡回籠覺時會說 go back to sleep。

如果利用逐字翻譯，我們要如何讓外國人理解「嫦娥奔月」的意思？只有字面直接翻譯這四個字外國人大概很難理解，由於這四個字牽涉嫦娥的神話故事，我們需要先解釋嫦娥這個人，然後為何要奔月（外國人形容月亮是空無一人的，我們則說月亮有兔子、有嫦娥，可熱鬧了），很多的文化或中文特有的意思是英文翻不出來的。

因此閱讀英文時應該避免一句英文一句中文翻譯的方式，因為兩種語言邏輯是不同的，思考方式也不同。可是台灣學生在學習英文閱讀時，往往淪為翻譯練習，執著於最貼切的單字翻譯。事實上，英文閱讀的能力並不會因為我們多認識了幾個單字而有所提升，如果有某個單字不認識時，我們不應該忙著先查字典，應該先試著了解那句話的語意。以下提供幾個例子讓讀者體會一下這兩種語言的文化差異。舉例來說：

文化背景的不同讓東西方對色彩有不同認知、聯想與意涵，東方常以紅色象徵喜氣、吉利、幸運，與好的事情（例如：紅包）。西方卻覺得紅色表示「危險」或是「警示」的意思（例如：a red flag），因此，紅色所代表的意思不同。以股票市場的漲跌顏色為例，在台灣，股票上漲用的是紅色，表示好運的喜氣（例如：股市長紅、台股收紅、台股一片紅通通）當台灣的股票下跌的時候，則用綠色來表示（例如：台股一片綠油油，投資人的臉都綠了）。

然而，美國與英國的股市漲跌顏色卻跟台灣是相反的。他們用綠色代表股票上漲，用紅色代表下跌，所以當美股一片綠油油的時候其實是表示股票上漲，因為綠色代表安全，紅色卻是危險。在翻譯的時候，必須要考慮這層文化的差異。

顏色所代表的文化差異也在其他的詞語方面顯現，例如英文用綠色表示妒嫉的意思，舉例來說 I am green with envy 或是 the green-eyed monster 就被比喻為妒嫉之意。相反地，中文常用「眼紅」來形容羨慕與妒嫉之心。因此中英文的妒嫉在色彩的文化聯想上面並不相同。

因為東西方文化的差異，所以對於許多比喻有不同的表達方式，舉例來說，英文形容出生在富貴家庭的小孩，會說 born with a silver spoon in one's mouth 是不是聽起來很熟悉呢？這句英文就是中文所說的「含著金湯匙出生」，中文說金湯匙，而英文說銀湯匙，同樣都是生於富貴之家的意思。

為何中文不是說「含著銀湯匙出生」？這主要是因為對中文的文化而言，黃金的價值明顯高於銀製品的緣故。在英文中，銀湯匙在文化傳統上面代表著富裕的意思，指家族富有或擁有貴族背景，因為中世紀時，一般平民只買得起木製餐具，只有皇室貴族或富裕商人才用得起銀製餐具，如銀湯匙、銀叉子、銀盤子等。自然而然，銀湯匙便成了富裕背景的象徵。

我們用「雨後春筍」形容某個現象或東西蓬勃發展，像是，手搖飲店如雨後春筍般在台北各地迅速增加，英文則是說 spring up like mushrooms 形容某件事情像是菇類一樣能夠迅速增加。都是迅速增加的意思，中文用筍來比喻，英文用菇來比喻。

中英文對於動物的聯想也不盡相同，舉例來說，當中文形容晚睡的人會說夜貓子，因為貓咪通常半夜是不太睡覺的，這對台灣許多貓奴來說是基本常識，可是，英文卻不是用貓這種動物來形容愛熬夜的人，英文會說 night owl 也就是貓頭鷹的意思，例如說 I am a night owl. 因為貓頭鷹是夜行性動物，晝伏夜出，晚上很活躍清醒，貓咪和貓頭鷹的共同點就是喜歡白天躲起來睡大覺。

英文以 chicken 表示怯弱膽小，例如 Don't be such a chicken，中文卻是說某人膽小如「鼠」。也就是說，中英文對於膽小的文化聯想是不同的。英文用雞來形容膽小是因為雞很容易受到驚嚇，當雞受到驚嚇時，會驚慌地拍動無法飛起來的雙翅，到處跑來跑去，貌似很膽小的樣子，所以chicken在英文中便有膽小怯弱的意思。

這些例子反映了我們對各種顏色、動物、意象所持有不同的想像，所以在學習英文時，我們必須考量並了解其文化背景和觀點。要正確理解英文，必須要意識到兩種語言之間的文化差異，以及在不同文化下，語言是如何的使用與詮釋。這種差異就如著名的紐約時報專欄作家 Flora Lewis 所形容："Learning another language is not only learning different words for the same things, but learning another way to think about things."

❷邏輯的差異

　　除了文化上的差異之外，這兩種語言的思維邏輯有時也是不同的，舉例來說，中文說「口香糖」，我們定義口香糖有味道，而且這個味道是香的。在英文中口香糖則叫做 chewing gum（翻譯：用來咀嚼的橡皮糖），英文定義口香糖是用來咀嚼的，香不香並不是英文定義此物的關鍵。

　　另一個例子就是中文所說的「奶嘴」英文稱為 pacifier（安撫物），中文強調奶嘴是取代乳頭的東西，英文卻認為奶嘴主要功能是用來安撫小寶寶的，中文取奶嘴的形象，英文取奶嘴的功能（附注：雖然近幾年來，台灣受英文影響甚多，越來越多人稱奶嘴為「安撫奶嘴」雖然漸漸加入了安撫的概念，但仍舊是以奶嘴為核心的主體）。

　　類似的還有「紅綠燈」，中文用形象來命名紅綠燈（因為早期紅綠燈只有兩色，沒有黃燈，否則中文可能稱之為紅綠黃燈了），在英文中卻是以紅綠燈的功能來命名之，英文叫做 traffic light，因為紅綠燈的功能為調節交通用，故英文稱「交通燈號」。

　　當形容一個人的言論缺乏深度，我們會說很「膚淺」，英文卻是用 skin-deep 來形容膚淺，也就是只有皮膚這麼「深」而已。雖然是用 deep 而不是 shallow, skin-deep 仍表示膚淺的意思。

　　有時候從英文而來的名詞被中文的思維邏輯所影響，甚至被曲解，舉例來說，在國外受教育 critical thinking 是很核心的一環，漸漸地，台灣的教室也常常聽到這個英文詞，中文常常翻譯為「批判性思考」，但此翻譯不但不適當，更常常誤導台灣學生對這個詞的認知，以為 critical thinking 就是要提出批評，因為是「批判性」思考，然而，這是不適當的翻譯產生了錯誤的中文思維。事實上，critical thinking 更為適當的翻譯應為「思辨能力」而非「批判性思考」，因為 critical thinking 是指具備檢視邏輯合理性的能力，因此能夠分析證據，論證並評估優劣，最後做出較為客觀的判斷與結論。「批判性」思考只片面地翻譯了「劣」的部分，卻沒有點出能夠看到「優」的部分也是 critical thinking 不可或缺的涵義。

　　在學術研究中也常常可以看到中英文思考邏輯的差異，舉例來說，一篇科學研究論文的最後通常會說「我們需要進行更進一步的研究」，但是英文卻不是說 We need further research 而是說 Further research is needed，為何英文將「研究」放在主詞的重要位置呢？這是因為在英文的邏輯中，「研究」比「誰」去做這個研究更重要，畢竟在科學研究中，主角是研究的主題，並非進行研究的人。因此，了解中英文思考邏輯的差異能夠讓我們更理解英文的表達方式，順序等。

❸文法的差異

　　中文跟英文有很多的文法差異，英文動詞有時態，而不同時態，有時候拼字也會改變（例如：write, wrote, written, writing）。另外，英文常使用被動語態，中文卻很少用被動語態，舉例來說，中文可以說，全世界都說英文（主動），英文則是 English is spoken all over the world. （被動）。中文不會說「英文在世界各地被說」。

　　或者另一個例子，中文可以說，這封信昨天寄出去了（主動），這句中文沒有顯示被動的意思，雖然我們當然知道信件是「被」寄出去的，在英文中就需要明確表達「被寄出去」這個動作，所以英文會說 This letter was mailed yesterday. （被動）。如果中文使用被動式──「這封信昨天被寄出去了」，則相當地不自然。

　　另外一個常見的文法差異就是詞性。就我在台大教書多年的觀察，台灣學生普遍對於詞性是不敏感的，所以常有用錯詞性的狀況發生，可能是因為在中文裡，詞性並不是那麼重要，但英文卻是很重要的，舉例來說，台灣常常會有學生將response 當動詞使用，雖然他們也認識 respond 這個字，這可能是因為這兩個字在中文都是「回應」的意思，像是「他們回應了這個問題」或「我們終於等到了他的回應」。詞性不同對中文通常不會有語意的差別，但是英文即便是同樣的一個字，有時候因為詞性不同，意思也會跟著改變，下面以常見的幾個單字舉例：

approach	n. 方法	v. 接近
show	n. 表演	v. 顯示
age	n. 年齡	v. 變老
park	n. 公園	v. 停車
house	n. 房子	v. 安置
book	n. 書	v. 預訂
table	n. 桌子	v. 擱置（議案等）
level	n. 程度	v. 夷平
leverage	n. 影響力	v. 利用
study	n. 研究	v. 學習
school	n. 學校	v. 教育
pen	n. 筆	v. 寫

另外，中文的形容詞必然放在名詞前面（例如：好漂亮的衣服=形容詞名詞），英文則有前置形容詞與後置形容詞兩種可能性（形容詞 + 名詞／名詞 + 形容詞），舉例來說：

He is a responsible person. 意思為「他是個負責任的人」，但若是將形容詞 responsible 移到 person 的後面：

He is the person responsible for this accident. 意思則為：「他就是造成這次意外的人」。

此外，英文的副詞，如果擺放的位置不同，有時候整句的意思也會改變，舉例來說：

Happily, he did not die. 意思為「還好他沒有死」。

但若是將 happily 移到最後面：

He did not die happily. 意思則變成 「他沒能善終」。

由這幾個例子可以看出中、英文的文法差異有時候會造成語意上的不同，想要提升英文理解力，對中文、英文的文法差異必須要有基本的概念。本書設計一套適合台灣學生的「高理解英文速讀」，利用台灣學生學習英文的經驗，幫助學生提升英文理解力。

第三堂課

測驗你的閱讀速度

這堂課要討論你的閱讀速度，包括：

- -1- 英文閱讀速度分級參考
- -2- 測驗你的「每分鐘有效閱讀速度」
- -3- 計算你的平均「每分鐘有效閱讀速度」

❶ 英文閱讀速度分級參考

　　母語人士正常說話一分鐘約 150 字左右。閱讀速度通常能夠比說話的速度快一點，受過大學以上教育的英文母語人士或是英文程度很高的台灣學生「每分鐘有效閱讀速度」大約能夠達到 250 字左右。但是大部分的台灣學生「每分鐘有效閱讀速度」大約只有 100 到 150 字左右。

　　所謂「每分鐘有效閱讀速度」Effective Words-Per-Minute （EWPM），就是 how fast you read with comprehension 也就是說，在完全看懂每句的前提下（不只是「看見」每個英文字而已），一分鐘能夠讀懂多少英文字。英文閱讀速度的參考分級如下表：

英文閱讀速度參考分級表

100–200 EWPM	You are a slow reader. (at talking speed)
200–300 EWPM	You are an average reader. (college-level native English speakers)
300–400 EWPM	You are an above-average reader.
400–600 EWPM	You are a fast reader, bravo!
600 EWPM+	Not recommended. Words may be coming at you faster than your mind can comprehend.

　　「每分鐘有效閱讀速度」 100-200 字表示閱讀速度過於緩慢，大約與自己說英文的速度差不多。具備大學教育水準的母語人士一分鐘大多能夠達到 200-300 字。如果一分鐘能夠達到 300-400 字，則已經是中上的閱讀水平。一分鐘 400-600 字代表英文閱讀實力相當堅強，閱讀效率高。那超過一分鐘 600 字呢？如同我在第一課「英文速讀的 NG 觀念」所指出，人類的視野是

有限的，過快的速度會讓視線變得模糊，感覺上有如走馬看花，無法做到有效閱讀。

❷測驗你的「每分鐘有效閱讀速度」

接下來的 5 頁共有 5 篇文章，閱讀每篇文章的時間只有 60 秒，請設定鬧鐘，60 秒時間一到，請停止閱讀，並標記停止閱讀的位置，然後計算已經閱讀的字數，計算完閱讀字數之後，請開始重新計時 60 秒，然後開始閱讀下一篇，以此類推，一篇只能閱讀 60 秒，所以閱讀完這 5 篇的時間總共為 5 分鐘。

★請注意，在閱讀下面這 5 篇文章時，必須要看懂每句的意思（不只是「看見」每個字而已）。

◎【第 1 篇】

All pop artists like to say that they owe their success to their fans. In the case of British band SVM, it's indeed true. The band is currently recording songs because 358 fans contributed the £100,000 needed for the project. The arrangement came via MMC, an online record label that uses Web-based, social-network-style "crowd-funding" to finance its acts.

Here's how it works: MMC posts demos and videos of 10 artists on its website, and users are invited to invest from £10 to £1,000 in the ones they most enjoy or think are most likely to become popular. Once an act reaches £100,000, the financing process is completed, and the money is used to pay for recording and possibly a concert tour. Profits from resulting music sales, concerts, and merchandise are split three ways: investors get to divide 40%; another 40% goes to MMC; the artist pockets 20%. The payoff for investors can be big. One fan in France who contributed £4,250 got his money back 22 times over.

Crowd-funding musical acts is not new. But MMC takes the concept to another level. First of all, investors can get cash rather than just goodies like free downloads or tickets. Also, MMC is a record label. It has the means to get its music distributed around the world and to market artists effectively. "Artists need professional support," says the CEO of MMC's international division.

While digital technology and the Net have created a do-it-yourself boom among musicians, success is still a long shot. Out of the 20,000 records released in the U.S. in 2009, only 14 DIY acts made it to the Top 200. Also, with less revenue from recorded music, music companies have become less likely to take risks, which has led to fewer artists receiving funding. The crowd-funding model, however, allows for more records to be made by spreading risk among hundreds of backers. And the social-network aspect of the site helps expand fan bases; that is, investors become a promotional army.

（102 年學測）

◎【第 2 篇】

American cooking programs have taught audiences, changed audiences, and changed with audiences from generation to generation. In October 1926, the U.S. Department of Agriculture created this genre's first official representative, a fictional radio host named Aunt Sammy. Over the airwaves, she educated homemakers on home economics and doled out advice on all kinds of matters, but it was mostly the cooking recipes that got listeners' attention. The show provided a channel for transmitting culinary advice and brought about a national exchange of recipes.

Cooking shows transitioned to television in the 1940s, and in the 1950s were often presented by a cook systematically explaining instructions on how to prepare dishes from start to finish. These programs were broadcast during the day and aimed at middle-class women whose mindset leaned toward convenient foods for busy families. Poppy Cannon, for example, was a popular writer of The Can-Opener Cookbook. She appeared on various television shows, using canned foods to demonstrate how to cook quickly and easily.

Throughout the sixties and seventies, a few chef-oriented shows redefined the genre as an exhibition of haute European cuisine by celebrity gourmet experts. This elite cultural aura then gave way to various cooking styles from around the world. An example of such change can be seen in Martin Yan's 1982 "Yan Can Cook" series, which demonstrated Chinese cuisine cooking with the catchphrase, "If Yan can cook, you can too!" By the 1990s, these cooking shows ranged from high-culture to health-conscious cuisine, with chefs' personalities and entertainment value being two keys to successful productions.

At the beginning of the 21st century, new cooking shows emerged to satisfy celeb-hungry, reality-crazed audiences. In this new millennium of out-of-studio shows and chef competition reality shows, chefs have become celebrities whose fame rivals that of rock stars. Audiences of these shows tend to be people who are interested in food and enjoy watching people cook rather than those who want to do the cooking themselves, leaving the age-old emphasis on following recipes outmoded.

（105 年指考）

◎【第 3 篇】

West Nile is a tropical disease that begins in birds, which pass it on to mosquitoes that then go on to infect human beings with a bite. Most people who contract West Nile do not experience any symptoms at all, but, if they do, symptoms typically develop between 3 to 14 days after a mosquito bite. About 1 in 5 persons suffers fever, headaches, and body aches, usually lasting a week or so. A far less lucky 1 in 150 experiences high fever, tremors, paralysis, and coma. Some—especially the elderly and those with weak immune systems—die.

That is what made the major outbreaks of West Nile in the U.S. in the summer of 2012 so scary. The situation was particularly bad in Dallas, Texas, where the West Nile virus killed 10 people and sickened more than 200. The city declared a state of emergency and began aerial spraying of a pesticide to kill the mosquitoes, even though residents argued that the pesticide could be more dangerous than the disease.

Why was the summer of 2012 so hospitable to the West Nile virus and the mosquitoes that carry it? Blame the weather. An extremely mild winter allowed more mosquitoes than usual to survive, while the unusually high temperatures in that scorching summer further increased their number by speeding up their life cycle. The economic crisis may have also played a role: Homeowners who were not able to pay their bank loans were forced to abandon their properties, sometimes leaving behind swimming pools that made excellent mosquito breeding grounds.

The severity of tropical diseases is also a matter of whether governments are capable—and willing— to defend their populations against infections. Dallas County was not doing some of the key things to slow the spread of West Nile, such as testing dead birds and setting mosquito traps to test for the presence of the disease. Tropical infections are thus as much related to government inaction as they are to climate.

（107 年學測）

◎【第4篇】

During the past three hundred years, when a country gains its freedom or independence, one of the first things established is a national anthem. National anthems are generally played and sung at formal state occasions and other events which celebrate or support the country's national identity.

Holland's 16th-century hymn "Het Wilhelmus" is widely considered the world's oldest national anthem, followed by the U.K.'s "God Save the King/Queen"—also a hymn, popularized in the 1740s. As nationalism spread throughout Europe in the 18th and 19th centuries, so did anthems. Many countries, such as the independent states that are today part of Germany, took "God Save the King/Queen" as a model and adopted hymns (songs of prayer typically addressed to a deity or VIP). Others, notably Spain and France, chose marches (songs with a strong, regular rhythm often performed by military bands)—which expressed a martial rather than monarchic spirit. With imperialism, Europeans spread their musical taste. Even when former colonies gained independence, they often imitated the traditions of their former rulers. The result is that most anthems are either hymns or marches, played on European instruments.

Japan's anthem makes for a good case study of European influence. In the 1860s a British bandmaster living in Japan, John William Fenton, noted that the country did not have a national anthem. A local military officer, Ōyama Iwao, selected the lyrics from a Heian era poem and Fenton wrote the melody. About a decade later, a Japanese committee chose a replacement melody by a court musician—one that had been composed for traditional Japanese instruments, but in a mixed style influenced by Fenton's arrangement. The version in use today was also altered by German Franz Eckert to fit a Western scale.

In addition to hymns and marches, British composer Michael Bristow identifies a couple of more minor categories. National anthems in South and Central America are often operatic, with long, elaborate orchestral introductions. These were influenced by 19th-century Italian opera. Burma and Sri Lanka are both in a folk group, as they rely more on indigenous instruments.

（106 年指考）

◎【第5篇】

Flickering lamps can induce headaches. But if the flickering happens millions of times a second—far faster than the eye can see or the brain process—then it might be harnessed to do something useful, like transmitting data. This is the idea behind Li-Fi, or Light Fidelity. The term Li-Fi was coined by University of Edinburgh Professor Harald Haas in a 2011 TED Talk, where he introduced the idea of "wireless data from every light." Today, Li-Fi has developed into a wireless technology that allows data to be sent at high speeds, working with light-emitting diodes (LEDs), an increasingly popular way to illuminate public areas and homes.

Using LED lights as networking devices for data transmission, Li-Fi has several advantages over Wi-Fi (Wireless Fidelity). First, Li-Fi allows for greater security on local networks, as light cannot penetrate walls or doors, unlike radio waves used in Wi-Fi. As long as transparent materials like glass windows are covered, access to a Li-Fi channel is limited to devices inside the room, ensuring that signals cannot be hacked from remote locations. Also, Li-Fi can operate in electromagnetic sensitive areas such as aircraft cabins, hospitals, and nuclear power plants, for light does not interfere with radio signals. The most significant advantage of Li-Fi is speed. Researchers have achieved speeds of 224 gigabits per second in lab conditions, much faster than Wi-Fi broadband.

How could Li-Fi enrich daily life? Anywhere there is LED lighting, there is an opportunity for Li-Fi enabled applications. Li-Fi-enabled street lights could provide internet access to mobile phones, making walking at night safer. The LED bulbs in traffic lights could provide drivers with weather conditions and traffic updates. Li-Fi could help with tourism by providing an easier access to local information. At home, smart light could also provide parents with solutions to their children's Internet addiction: Just turn off the lights and you've turned off their access.

When 14 billion light bulbs mean 14 billion potential transmitters of wireless data, a cleaner, a greener, and even a brighter future is on the way.

（107 年指考）

❸計算你的平均「每分鐘有效閱讀速度」

	每分鐘有效閱讀速度 EWPM
第一篇	
第二篇	
第三篇	
第四篇	
第五篇	
五篇平均	

平均每分鐘有效閱讀速度 = 五篇 EWPM 總和 除以 5

第四堂課

如何提升英文閱讀理解力

許多因素可能會影響英文的閱讀理解力，包含學科的背景知識 (subject matter knowledge)、文體的背景知識(genre knowledge) 、詞彙知識(vocabulary knowledge)、思辨能力(critical thinking) 、以及對語意的掌握等。本書將會從英文語意的角度探討如何提升理解力，其他層面日後有機會再詳細討論。

-1- 傳統英文閱讀vs.高理解英文速讀
-2- 兩者理解方式的關鍵差異
-3- 提升理解力需要看見「有意義」的群組
-4- 英文有哪些「有意義」的群組？
-5- 隨堂測驗

❶傳統英文閱讀 vs. 高理解英文速讀

「傳統英文閱讀」的方式是一次看一個字 a word by a word，也就是一個字一個字逐字看，越看不懂越要一個字一個字看，但事實上，如同看電影一樣，就算一句台詞不太懂意思，整部電影仍然可以看懂，但若因為這一句台詞而停滯不前，對接下來的劇情完全視而不見的話，那就真的無法看懂整部電影了。

我用一個的簡單的句子示範「傳統英文閱讀」的方式：

A big dog is running through the park.

我們眼睛在看這個句子的時候，就像是下圖一樣，一次注視著一個單字：

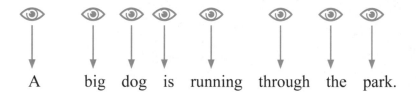

| A | big | dog | is | running | through | the | park. |

換言之，在試圖理解這短短的一個句子的時候，其實你就已經看了許多「次」了，只不過每次都是切開一個字一個字去理解的。用這樣的方法閱讀整篇文章自然會耗費相當多的時間，更重要的是，這樣一個字一個字看的閱讀方式耗時卻無法提升理解力。是沒有效率的閱讀方式。

「高理解英文速讀」並不是一個字一個字逐字閱讀，而是要看見「有意義」的群組，我以同一個句子作示範：

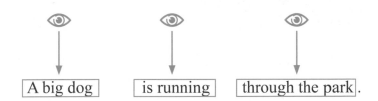

因為注視句中帶有意義的群組，所以同樣的句子只要三次就可以看完，並且能夠看見這三個在句中產生意義的群組。

讓我們再看一次這兩種閱讀方式，哪一種比較容易理解？

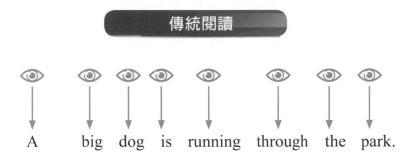

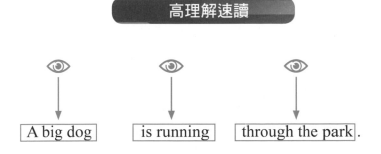

❷ 兩者理解方式的關鍵差異

因為「傳統英文閱讀」多以詞性作為理解的基本單位（詞性稱為 parts of speech；語言學家稱之 word classes ），英文的詞性包含：

名詞	noun (e.g., a car)
代名詞	pronoun (e.g., her)
動詞	verb (e.g., learn)
形容詞	adjective (e.g., happy)
副詞	adverb (e.g., happily)
介係詞	preposition (e.g., in)
連接詞	conjunction (e.g., because)
冠詞	article (e.g., the)

用同一個簡單的句子做說明：

A big dog is running through the park.

一個字一個字看的「傳統英文閱讀」包含這些文法單位（如下圖示）：

以詞性為基本理解單位							
A	**big**	**dog**	**is**	**running**	**through**	**the**	**park.**
article	adj	noun	verb	participle	prep	article	noun

也就是說，「傳統英文閱讀」著重每個單字的文法詞性（a focus on single, isolated words），在我們眼中顯示的即為名詞、動詞、介係詞、副詞、形容詞、冠詞、連接詞、代名詞等文法單位。但是，由於文法詞性本身是沒有實質意義的，因此這樣逐字閱讀時，句意無法快速連貫理解。

「高理解英文速讀」則是幫助學生看見文章的內容，並且理解產生這些內容的英文群組的意思，之所以能夠提升理解力，正是因為每一眼所看見的都是有意義的群組（a focus on meaningful units of text instead of single, isolated words）。例如： the boy in red shirt 是一個有意義的基本單位，而不是沒有意義關聯的 5 個分離單字（例如，the – boy –in – red – shirt 這 5 個分離單字），所以「高理解英文速讀」並不是一個字一個字看的。而是一組字一組字有意義地理解英文。也就是說每次看見的都是a meaningful unit of text。

舉另外一個例子來說，driving rain 的意義若單獨分開看driving 和 rain兩個字，則無法正確理解driving rain這組字的意思。「高理解英文速讀」的目標是幫助學生看見 meaningful units of text 與 a flow of ideas，如此才能夠有感提升英文理解力和速度。2019 年劍橋線上字典的網站也宣揚類似的語言學習理念："Make your words meaningful"。

那何謂看到有意義的群組呢？我以同一個句子作為示範：

A big dog is running through the park.

以有意義的群組為基本理解單位		
A big dog	**is running**	**through the park.**
what	action	where

也就是說 A big dog 作為一個 WHAT 的意義單位。動作單位 ACTION 即為 is running。在哪裡做這個動作呢？WHERE 這個地點單位即為 through the park。這樣的方式理解這個句子，英文好像變簡單了，一個句子只需看 2~3 次，而且能夠獲得較高的理解力，相反地，「傳統英文閱讀」需要一個字一個字地看，一個句子至少需要看 10 次以上，因此每一個句子都多停留了幾秒鐘，一篇文章下來，自然耗費更多時間，然而，耗費更多的時間卻無法獲得較好的理解力，因此事倍功半。

❸ 提升理解力需要看見「有意義」的群組

以下幾個例子示範如何看見「有意義」的群組：

❶ One slippery seal was building fences.

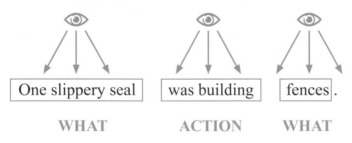

One slippery seal	was building	fences.
WHAT	**ACTION**	**WHAT**

❷ The shy puppy is hiding under the bed.

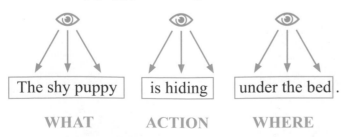

The shy puppy	is hiding	under the bed.
WHAT	**ACTION**	**WHERE**

❸ In winter, the orange leaves are falling.

In winter,	the orange leaves	are falling.
WHEN	**WHAT**	**ACTION**

❹ Beside the ice cream truck, the little girl is shouting.

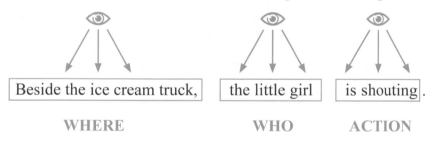

Beside the ice cream truck,	the little girl	is shouting.
WHERE	**WHO**	**ACTION**

❺ The girl in the spotty hat was painting motorbikes in the morning.

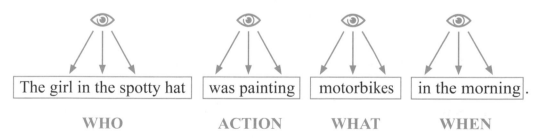

The girl in the spotty hat	was painting	motorbikes	in the morning.
WHO	**ACTION**	**WHAT**	**WHEN**

　　接下來，以 106 年學測閱讀的第一個段落作為示範，讓讀者感受一下「傳統英文閱讀」和「高理解英文速讀」在實際閱讀時的差異感受。

傳統閱讀

Capoeira is a martial art that combines elements of fight, acrobatics, drumming, singing, dance, and rituals. It involves a variety of techniques that make use of the hands, feet, legs, arms, and head. Although Capoeira appears dancelike, many of its basic techniques are similar to those in other martial arts.

Capoeira **is** a martial art that combines elements of fight, acrobatics, drumming, singing, dance, and rituals. It involves a variety of techniques that make use of the hands, feet, legs, arms, and head. Although Capoeira appears dancelike, many of its basic techniques are similar to those in other martial arts.

Capoeira is **a** martial art that combines elements of fight, acrobatics, drumming, singing, dance, and rituals. It involves a variety of techniques that make use of the hands, feet, legs, arms, and head. Although Capoeira appears dancelike, many of its basic techniques are similar to those in other martial arts.

Capoeira is a **martial** art that combines elements of fight, acrobatics, drumming, singing, dance, and rituals. It involves a variety of techniques that make use of the hands, feet, legs, arms, and head. Although Capoeira appears dancelike, many of its basic techniques are similar to those in other martial arts.

Capoeira is a martial **art** that combines elements of fight, acrobatics, drumming, singing, dance, and rituals. It involves a variety of techniques that make use of the hands, feet, legs, arms, and head. Although Capoeira appears dancelike, many of its basic techniques are similar to those in other martial arts.

Capoeira is a martial art **that** combines elements of fight, acrobatics, drumming, singing, dance, and rituals. It involves a variety of techniques that make use of the hands, feet, legs, arms, and head. Although Capoeira appears dancelike, many of its basic techniques are similar to those in other martial arts.

Capoeira is a martial art that **combines** elements of fight, acrobatics, drumming, singing, dance, and rituals. It involves a variety of techniques that make use of the hands, feet, legs, arms, and head. Although Capoeira appears dancelike, many of its basic techniques are similar to those in other martial arts.

Capoeira is a martial art that combines **elements** of fight, acrobatics, drumming, singing, dance, and rituals. It involves a variety of techniques that make use of the hands, feet, legs, arms, and head. Although Capoeira appears dancelike, many of its basic techniques are similar to those in other martial arts.

Capoeira is a martial art that combines elements **of** fight, acrobatics, drumming, singing, dance, and rituals. It involves a variety of techniques that make use of the hands, feet, legs, arms, and head. Although Capoeira appears dancelike, many of its basic techniques are similar to those in other martial arts.

Capoeira is a martial art that combines elements of **fight**, acrobatics, drumming, singing, dance, and rituals. It involves a variety of techniques that make use of the hands, feet, legs, arms, and head. Although Capoeira appears dancelike, many of its basic techniques are similar to those in other martial arts.

Capoeira is a martial art that combines elements of fight, **acrobatics**, drumming, singing, dance, and rituals. It involves a variety of techniques that make use of the hands, feet, legs, arms, and head. Although Capoeira appears dancelike, many of its basic techniques are similar to those in other martial arts.

Capoeira is a martial art that combines elements of fight, acrobatics, drumming , singing, dance, and rituals. It involves a variety of techniques that make use of the hands, feet, legs, arms, and head. Although Capoeira appears dancelike, many of its basic techniques are similar to those in other martial arts.

Capoeira is a martial art that combines elements of fight, acrobatics, drumming, singing , dance, and rituals. It involves a variety of techniques that make use of the hands, feet, legs, arms, and head. Although Capoeira appears dancelike, many of its basic techniques are similar to those in other martial arts.

Capoeira is a martial art that combines elements of fight, acrobatics, drumming, singing, dance , and rituals. It involves a variety of techniques that make use of the hands, feet, legs, arms, and head. Although Capoeira appears dancelike, many of its basic techniques are similar to those in other martial arts.

高理解速讀

Capoeira is a martial art that combines elements of fight, acrobatics, drumming, singing, dance, and rituals. It involves a variety of techniques that make use of the hands, feet, legs, arms, and head. Although Capoeira appears dancelike, many of its basic techniques are similar to those in other martial arts.

Capoeira is a martial art that combines elements of fight, acrobatics, drumming, singing, dance, and rituals. It involves a variety of techniques that make use of the hands, feet, legs, arms, and head. Although Capoeira appears dancelike, many of its basic techniques are similar to those in other martial arts.

Capoeira is a martial art **that combines** elements of fight, acrobatics, drumming, singing, dance, and rituals. It involves a variety of techniques that make use of the hands, feet, legs, arms, and head. Although Capoeira appears dancelike, many of its basic techniques are similar to those in other martial arts.

Capoeira is a martial art that combines **elements of** fight, acrobatics, drumming, singing, dance, and rituals. It involves a variety of techniques that make use of the hands, feet, legs, arms, and head. Although Capoeira appears dancelike, many of its basic techniques are similar to those in other martial arts.

Capoeira is a martial art that combines elements of **fight, acrobatics, drumming, singing, dance, and rituals** . It involves a variety of techniques that make use of the hands, feet, legs, arms, and head. Although Capoeira appears dancelike, many of its basic techniques are similar to those in other martial arts.

Capoeira is a martial art that combines elements of fight, acrobatics, drumming, singing, dance, and rituals. **It** involves a variety of techniques that make use of the hands, feet, legs, arms, and head. Although Capoeira appears dancelike, many of its basic techniques are similar to those in other martial arts.

Capoeira is a martial art that combines elements of fight, acrobatics, drumming, singing, dance, and rituals. It **involves** a variety of techniques that make use of the hands, feet, legs, arms, and head. Although Capoeira appears dancelike, many of its basic techniques are similar to those in other martial arts.

Capoeira is a martial art that combines elements of fight, acrobatics, drumming, singing, dance, and rituals. It involves **a variety of techniques** that make use of the hands, feet, legs, arms, and head. Although Capoeira appears dancelike, many of its basic techniques are similar to those in other martial arts.

Capoeira is a martial art that combines elements of fight, acrobatics, drumming, singing, dance, and rituals. It involves a variety of techniques **that make use of** the hands, feet, legs, arms, and head. Although Capoeira appears dancelike, many of its basic techniques are similar to those in other martial arts.

Capoeira is a martial art that combines elements of fight, acrobatics, drumming, singing, dance, and rituals. It involves a variety of techniques that make use of **the hands, feet, legs, arms, and head** . Although Capoeira appears dancelike, many of its basic techniques are similar to those in other martial arts.

Capoeira is a martial art that combines elements of fight, acrobatics, drumming, singing, dance, and rituals. It involves a variety of techniques that make use of the hands, feet, legs, arms, and head. **Although** Capoeira appears dancelike, many of its basic techniques are similar to those in other martial arts.

Capoeira is a martial art that combines elements of fight, acrobatics, drumming, singing, dance, and rituals. It involves a variety of techniques that make use of the hands, feet, legs, arms, and head. Although **Capoeira** appears dancelike, many of its basic techniques are similar to those in other martial arts.

Capoeira is a martial art that combines elements of fight, acrobatics, drumming, singing, dance, and rituals. It involves a variety of techniques that make use of the hands, feet, legs, arms, and head. Although Capoeira **appears dancelike** , many of its basic techniques are similar to those in other martial arts.

Capoeira is a martial art that combines elements of fight, acrobatics, drumming, singing, dance, and rituals. It involves a variety of techniques that make use of the hands, feet, legs, arms, and head. Although Capoeira appears dancelike, **many of its basic techniques** are similar to those in other martial arts.

Capoeira is a martial art that combines elements of fight, acrobatics, drumming, singing, dance, and rituals. It involves a variety of techniques that make use of the hands, feet, legs, arms, and head. Although Capoeira appears dancelike, many of its basic techniques **are similar to** those in other martial arts.

Capoeira is a martial art that combines elements of fight, acrobatics, drumming, singing, dance, and rituals. It involves a variety of techniques that make use of the hands, feet, legs, arms, and head. Although Capoeira appears dancelike, many of its basic techniques are similar to **those in other martial arts**.

　　由上面的示範段落可以看出，「傳統英文閱讀」看了 14 次都還無法看完第一句，「高理解英文速讀」只看了 16 次就看完了整個段落（共三句），由於注視著有意義的英文群組，所以能夠更清楚地理解文意的發展（flow of ideas），有感提升英文理解力。

❹英文有哪些有意義的群組？

「高理解英文速讀」讓我們看見有意義的英文群組，這些有意義的群組在英文句子中通常會執行一個明確的功能，如下表：

有意義的群組 (meaningful unit)	定義 (definition)	文法結構 (syntactic realizations)	舉例 (examples)
WHO/WHAT	人物、抽象概念、現象、行動或行為	名詞群組等 Nominal groups, etc.	① Beer cans ② The lower layers of the sea
ACTION	表示動作的全部動詞（含助動詞）	動詞群組 Verbal groups	① They picked up stones. ② We turned over every stone.
CIRCUMSTANCE	表示狀態的副詞或介系詞片語	副詞群組 Adverbial groups 介系詞群組 Prepositional groups	① In the room ② On the 7th of October

「高理解英文速讀」從語意的角度出發，主要強調三種群組，第一種是WHO/WHAT (WHO即是人，WHAT非人物)，例如: the lower layers of the sea即是WHAT的意思。

第二種是ACTION，這個群組用來表示動作的意思，動詞（包含助動詞）都在這個群組裡面（例如：They picked up stones）.

第三種是 CIRCUSTANCE 群組，這個群組表示時間，地點，做某事的方式等意思（例如：in the room）。接下來逐一介紹每個群組並舉例說明。

4.1 WHO/WHAT 群組

在 WHO/WHAT 的群組中，WHO 即為人物（單數或複數），而 WHAT 即為具體的非人物，抽象概念、現象、行動或行為，如下表：

WHO 群組

種類	舉例
單數的人物	a teacher, Michael Jordan, a tall guy, the driver, the basketball player, I, me, you, she, he, her, him, the brave girl holding her bag, a basketball player who won 6 NBA championships
複數的人物	people, more men, a teacher and her students, a group of students, us, ten of, humans, we, they, them

WHAT 群組

種類	舉例
具體的非人物	a big book, beer cans, one hundred flies, a dog, a spicy stew, the lower layers of the sea, a blue umbrella with a black handle, John's new bike, the dark old house, a murderer's finger marks, a box, an alley, the car
抽象概念、現象、行動或行為	good ideas, the baking of cakes, a funny feeling, the art of business, a vicious circle, a problem, a concept, an issue, results, a process, a reason, racism, the exploration of the cosmos

WHO 為人物（單數或複數），例如 Michael Jordan（單數人物）或 a teacher and her students （複數人物）。WHAT 則包含具體非人物、抽象概念、現象或行動／行為，例如beer cans （具體非人物），the exploration of the cosmos（行動）。

4.2 ACTION 群組

ACTION 群組表達動作的意思，在文法上這個群組包含了助動詞及所有動詞。這個群組主要的意思為：ACTION, HAVING, BEING, FEELING, SAYING。種類與例子如下表：

種類	舉例
ACTION	He snatched up sticks and stones. They picked up stones. The greedy dinosaur is eating bicycles. Two cuddly koalas are sleeping.
HAVING	Kevin has a beautiful bike. I had some books. Sha really has a lot of good ideas.
BEING	Ingrid is an English teacher. Kevin was fantastic on the game. He was friendly. The flowers are lovely.

FEELING	I hate her curly hair.
	Her curly hair amazed me.
	I ignored the rest.
	The students liked the English teacher.
SAYING	Mike said nothing.
	'Listen!' Mike shouted.
	'Did you hear him?' I asked.
	'See you later,' he whispered.

　　ACTION 包含一般的動作，例如 They picked up stones. 中的 ACTION 就是 picked up。HAVING 則是擁有相關的意思，例如 Kevin has a beautiful bike. 中的 HAVING 就是 has。BEING 則是表達形容一種身分或狀態，所以通常與名詞或形容詞組合成為 BEING 的意思，例如 The flowers are lovely. 中的 BEING 就是 are lovely 的個可愛的狀態。FEELING 是指人的感受，例如 The students liked the English teacher. 中 liked 就是喜歡的這種感受。最後一個則是 SAYING，很多種文章都會引述某人說的話，此時的動作則是 SAYING，例如 'Did you hear him?' I asked. 中 asked 就是 SAYING 說了什麼話的意思。

4.3 ACTION 與 WHAT 的角色互換

　　ACTION 跟 WHAT 有時候可以依據文意需要而互換腳色，此互換腳色稱為「名詞化的動詞」（Nominalization），如下圖示：

ACTION	➡ WHAT
Superman dies .	The death of Superman
A bomb exploded .	The explosion of a bomb
The German forces were defeated .	The defeat of Germany
New environmental factors are introduced .	The introduction of new environmental factors
A component disappears .	The disappearance of a component
An ecosystem collapses .	The collapse of an ecosystem

　　之所以稱為名詞化的動詞是因為文法上已經轉變成名詞了，例如 The bomb exploded 中的 exploded 是爆炸的意思，當爆炸這個意思轉變成名詞的時候（explosion）就稱為「名詞化的動詞」，也就是說exploded（ACTION）這個動作已經轉化成為 explosion（WHAT），不再是 ACTION 的意思了。

4.4 CIRCUMSTANCE 群組

　　除了 WHO / WHAT 與 ACTION 群組之外，最後一個群組就是 CIRCUMSTANCE 群組，在文法上這個群組包含了副詞、副詞片語、介係詞片語。

種類	舉例
WHERE	Mike tore his shorts in the park . She ate the cake in the car . We will read it in the final chapter . There was blood on his clothes .
WHEN	The park is popular on summer nights . He decided to apologize later on . He woke up the next morning . At first she didn't notice me.
HOW	Mr. Brown tore his shorts carelessly . The dog began to sniff suspiciously . I checked my answers carefully . Kyle chained the dog up securely .
HOW OFTEN	The dog sniffed at the box twice . He goes to school five days a week .
WHY	He tore his shorts for fun . They write in order to provide a summary .
WITH WHOM/WHAT	Mike was having lunch with his girlfriend . The lizard snapped at many flies with its long tongue .
AS WHO/WHAT	He seemed to take his own instinct as a huge joke . She came here to give a talk as President .

　　CIRCUMSTANCE 群組包含 WHERE, WHEN, HOW, HOW OFTEN, WHY, WITH WHOM/WHAT, FOR WHOM/WHAT, AS WHO/WHAT。

　　WHERE 就是地點，例如：She ate the cake in the car 中的 in the car 這

個地點就是 WHERE。WHEN 是時間，例如：The park is popular on summer nights 中的 on summer nights 這個時間就是 WHEN 的意思。HOW 是執行動作的方式，例如：I checked my answers carefully 中的 carefully（仔細地）就是 HOW 的意思，用來表達 checked my answers 的方式。HOW OFTEN 是頻率的意思，例如 He goes to school five days a week 中的 five days a week 就是頻率的意思。WHY 則是原因目的動機等，例如：Mike tore his shorts for fun 中的 for fun 即為目的的意思。WITH WHOM/WHAT 的例子 The lizard snapped at many flies with its long tongue 中 with its long tongue 即蜥蜴用什麼東西逮到蒼蠅的意思。AS WHO/WHAT 是作為什麼身分或當作何事的意思，例如：He seemed to take his own instinct as a huge joke 中 as a huge joke 就是當作一個大笑話的意思。

4.5 沒有實質意義的虛位主詞

英文的語言結構必須要有主詞的存在（除了祈使句之外，例如 Stand up now!），雖然主詞通常是 WHO 或 WHAT 的意思，然而，並不是所有主詞都能夠產生實質的意思，這種沒有實質意思的主詞稱為「虛位主詞」。英文中就有兩種虛位主詞（即為 IT & THERE），IT 與 THERE 做為虛位主詞的時候並不具備任何實質的意思（只是虛占其位而已），英文語法結構上需要這個虛位主詞的存在，語言學家稱之為 a dummy subject 或 a semantically empty subject 或 a grammatical place-holder。以 IT 舉例來說：

❶ It　is an honor　to see the movie star.

　　　　BEING　　　　WHAT

❷ It　is important　that we read more efficiently.

　　　　BEING　　　　WHAT

　　由❶、❷可以看出，真正具備意思的主詞（WHAT）其實在句子後面。
另外一個英文獨特的語法結構為 There is/There are。There 本身其實只是一個
副詞，但是當 There 占在主詞的位置時，There 即成為了一種虛位主詞，此
時，真正有意義的主詞其實在句子後面，這種實際主詞後置的語言結構稱為
postposition 或 extraposition。舉例來說：

❶ There were 　　ten of us　　　in the party.

　　　　　　　　　　WHO　　　　　WHERE

= **Ten of us were in the party.**

❷ There are 　　five students　　　in the classroom.

　　　　　　　　　WHO　　　　　　　WHERE

= **Five students are in the classroom.**

❸ There are 　　no flies　　in this kitchen.

　　　　　　　　　WHAT　　　WHERE

= **No flies are in this kitchen.**

❹ There are 　　plenty of fish　　　in the sea.

　　　　　　　　　WHAT　　　　　　WHERE

= **Plenty of fish are in the sea.**

❺ 隨堂測驗

請填入 WHO, ACTION, WHERE 等有意義的群組功能。

❶   I   am standing   on a beach.

　　_____   _____   _____

❷   Mike   opened   the door.

　　_____   _____   _____

❸   They   looked at   the running dog.

　　_____   _____   _____

❹   Annie and John   live   in New York.

　　_____   _____   _____

❺   I   told   her   the truth.

　　_____   _____   _____   _____

❻ His close friend   wrote   this book   in Taiwan.

_____   _____   _____   _____

❼ Annie   played   basketball   yesterday.

_____   _____   _____

❽ Bruce   swallowed   the ping pong ball   by mistake.

_____   _____   _____   _____

❾ One silly monkey   is swinging   in the trees.

_____   _____   _____

❿ My friend   was seized by   some of the crew.

_____   _____   _____

⑪ At the club,   I   drank   some beer and   ate   chips.

_____   _____   _____   _____   ___   _____

⑫ They   attacked   the village   and   killed

_____   _____   _____   _____

many people.

_____

⑬ These days,   many young people   use   Instagram.

_____   _____   ___   _____

⑭ Jenny   wanted to play   her new toy   in her room.

_____   _____   _____   _____

⑮ The big bear   is sleeping   inside its dark cave.

_____   _____   _____

⑯　　　Last week,　　　the dairy cow　　　was dancing　　　in my dream.

_____　_____　_____　_____

⑰　　　The fat bees　　　were buzzing　　　around the hive.

_____　_____　　　_____

⑱　　　In the deep dark woods,　　　the fluffy bunny　　　is bouncing.

_____　　　_____　　　_____

⑲　　　John　　　bought　　　a blue umbrella with a black handle.

_____　_____　_____

⑳　　　On the 7th of August,　　　Vivian's husband John

_____　　　_____

was reading　　　a book　　　in an apartment in New York.

_____　_____　_____

解答在第230頁

第五堂課

實戰練習（一）

練習❶

〈單字〉

❶ still
靜止不動的 (adj.)

【例句】 Sitting still for an hour can be difficult for young kids.

❷ perform on command
聽從指令做動作 (v.)

【例句】 It is very difficult to have a 2-year old perform on command.

❸ appealing
令人喜歡的 (adj.)

【例句】 Puppies are especially appealing to children.

❹ treat
喜歡的東西 (n.)

【例句】 In this party, cookies and tasty treats are provided.

請先花 5 秒鐘看看全文有多長即可 ⇨

練習①

Animals are a favorite subject of many photographers. Cats, dogs, and other pets top the list, followed by zoo animals. However, because it's hard to get them to sit still and "perform on command," some professional photographers refuse to photograph pets.

One way to get an appealing portrait of a cat or dog is to hold a biscuit or treat above the camera. The animal's longing look toward the food will be captured by the camera, but the treat won't appear in the picture because it's out of the camera's range. When you show the picture to your friends afterwards, they'll be impressed by your pet's loving expression.

If you are using fast film, you can take some good, quick shots of a pet by simply snapping a picture right after calling its name. You'll get a different expression from your pet using this technique. Depending on your pet's mood, the picture will capture an interested, curious expression or possibly a look of annoyance, especially if you've awakened it from a nap.

Taking pictures of zoo animals requires a little more patience. After all, you can't wake up a lion! You may have to wait for a while until the animal does something interesting or moves into a position for you to get a good shot. When photographing zoo animals, don't get too close to the cages, and never tap on the glass or throw things between the bars of a cage. Concentrate on shooting some good pictures, and always respect the animals you are photographing.

（107 年學測）

現在開始提升你的理解力吧！請翻到次頁，倒數計時 60 秒開始！

（第一段）

Animals are a favorite subject of many photographers. Cats, dogs, and other pets top the list, followed by zoo animals. However, because it is hard to get them to sit still and "perform on command," some professional photographers refuse to photograph pets.

Animals are a favorite subject of many photographers. Cats, dogs, and other pets top the list, followed by zoo animals. However, because it is hard to get them to sit still and "perform on command," some professional photographers refuse to photograph pets.

（第二段）

One way to get an appealing portrait of a cat or dog is to hold a biscuit or treat above the camera. The animal's longing look toward the food will be captured by thecamera, but the treat won't appear in the picture because it's out of the camera's range. When you show the picture to your friends afterwards, they'll be impressed by your pet's loving expression.

One way to get an appealing portrait of a cat or dog is to hold a biscuit or treat above the camera. The animal's longing look toward the food will be captured by the camera, but the treat won't appear in the picture because it's out of the camera's range. When you show the picture to your friends afterwards, they'll be impressed by your pet's loving expression.

One way to get an appealing portrait of a cat or dog is to hold a biscuit or treat above the camera. The animal's longing look toward the food will be captured by the camera, but the treat won't appear in the picture because it's out of the camera's range. When you show the picture to your friends afterwards, they 'll be impressed by your pet's loving expression.

（第三段）

If you are using fast film, you can take some good, quick shots of a pet by simply snapping a picture right after calling its name. You'll get a different expression from your pet using this technique. Depending on your pet's mood, the picture will capture an interested, curious expression or possibly a look of annoyance, especially if you've awakened it from a nap.

If you are using fast film, you can take some good, quick shots of a pet by simply snapping a picture right after calling its name. You 'll get a different expression from your pet using this technique. Depending on your pet's mood, the picture will capture an interested, curious expression or possibly a look of annoyance, especially if you've awakened it from a nap.

If you are using fast film, you can take some good, quick shots of a pet by simply snapping a picture right after calling its name. You'll get a different expression from your pet using this technique. Depending on your pet's mood, the picture will capture an interested, curious expression or possibly a look of annoyance , especially if you 've awakened it from a nap .

（第四段）

Taking pictures of zoo animals requires a little more patience . After all , you can't wake up a lion ! You may have to wait for a while until the animal does something interesting or moves into a position for you to get a good shot. When photographing zoo animals, don't get too close to the cages, and never tap on the glass or throw things between the bars of a cage. Concentrate on shooting some good pictures, and always respect the animals you are photographing.

Taking pictures of zoo animals requires a little more patience. After all, you can't wake up a lion! You may have to wait for a while until the animal does something interesting or moves into a position for you to get a good shot . When photographing zoo animals, don't get too close to the cages, and never tap on the glass or throw things between the bars of a cage. Concentrate on shooting some good pictures, and always respect the animals you are photographing.

Taking pictures of zoo animals requires a little more patience. After all, you can't wake up a lion! You may have to wait for a while until the animal does something interesting or moves into a position for you to get a good shot. When photographing zoo animals , don't get too close to the cages , and never tap on the glass or throw things between the bars of a cage . Concentrate on shooting some good pictures, and always respect the animals you are photographing.

Taking pictures of zoo animals requires a little more patience. After all, you can't wake up a lion! You may have to wait for a while until the animal does something interesting or moves into a position for you to get a good shot. When photographing zoo animals, don't get too close to the cages, and never tap on the glass or throw things between the bars of a cage. Concentrate on shooting some good pictures, and always respect the animals you are photographing.

　　　本書使用簡短的是非題直接檢視讀者對文章的理解力，檢驗讀者是否在 60 秒內對於文章核心知識有正確的理解力，是否誤解文意。以下的是非題不是正式的考題，因此不需要耗費大量時間思考即可回答，只要幾秒鐘即可完成。

依據文意，請判斷對錯。若是對的就在括弧內打 O，錯就打 X。
不確定是否正確時，請勿回答或猜測答案
（未回答的題目請計算為錯誤題數）

❶ (　　)

Cats and dogs are the most popular subjects of photographers.

❷ (　　)

The food and the animal will both appear in the picture.

❸ (　　)

People call their pet's name in order to make sure it sits still.

❹ (　　)

Taking pictures of family cats and dogs requires more patience than taking pictures of zoo animals.

❺ (　　)

Fast film allows you to take quick shots.

只花了 60 秒閱讀這篇文章，你答對了幾題？請對答案！
你的理解力＝(正確題數) 除以 5 再乘以 100%＝＿＿＿＿%

練習❷

〈單字〉

❶ the English royal court
　英國皇室 (n.)

　【例句】 Prince Harry is a member of the English royal court .

❷ beverage
　飲品 (n.)

　【例句】 You can find some beverages on the back of the menu.

❸ the nobility
　貴族 (n.)

　【例句】 Prince Harry is a member of the nobility .

❹ account for
　估計是 (v.)

　【例句】 People holding an undergraduate degree account for 25%
　　　　　 of the US population.

請先花 5 秒鐘看看全文有多長即可 ⇨

練習②

Tea, the most typical English drink, became established in Britain because of the influence of a foreign princess, Catherine of Braganza, the queen of Charles II. A lover of tea since her childhood in Portugal, she brought tea-drinking to the English royal court and set a trend for the beverage in the seventeenth century. The fashion soon spread beyond the circle of the nobility to the middle classes, and tea became a popular drink at the London coffee houses where people met to do business and discuss events of the day. Many employers served a cup of tea to their workers in the middle of the morning, thus inventing a lasting British institution, the "tea break." However, drinking tea in social settings outside the workplace was beyond the means of the majority of British people. It came with a high price tag and tea was taxed as well.

Around 1800, the seventh Duchess of Bedford, Anne Maria, began the popular practice of "afternoon tea," a ceremony taking place at about four o'clock. Until then, people did not usually eat or drink anything between lunch and dinner. At approximately the same time, the Earl of Sandwich popularized a new way of eating bread—in thin slices, with something (e.g., jam or cucumbers) between them. Before long, a small meal at the end of the afternoon, involving tea and sandwiches, had become part of the British way of life.

As tea became much cheaper during the nineteenth century, its popularity spread right through all corners of the British society. Thus, tea became Britain's favorite drink. In working-class households, it was served with the main meal of the day, eaten when workers returned home after a day's labor. This meal has become known as "high tea."

Today, tea can be drunk at any time of the day, and accounts for over two-fifths of all beverages consumed in Britain—with the exception of water.

（106 年學測）

現在開始提升你的理解力吧！倒數計時 60 秒開始！

（第一段）

Tea , the most typical English drink , became established in Britain because of the influence of a foreign princess , Catherine of Braganza, the queen of Charles II . A lover of tea since her childhood in Portugal, she brought tea-drinking to the English royal court and set a trend for the beverage in the seventeenth century. The fashion soon spread beyond the circle of the nobility to the middle classes, and tea became a popular drink at the London coffee houses where people met to do business and discuss events of the day. Many employers served a cup of tea to their workers in the middle of the morning, thus inventing a lasting British institution, the "tea break." However, drinking tea in social settings outside the workplace was beyond the means of the majority of British people. It came with a high price tag and tea was taxed as well.

Tea, the most typical English drink, became established in Britain because of the influence of a foreign princess, Catherine of Braganza, the queen of Charles II. A lover of tea since her childhood in Portugal , she brought tea-drinking to the English royal court and set a trend for the beverage in the seventeenth century . The fashion soon spread beyond the circle of the nobility to the middle classes, and tea became a popular drink at the London coffee houses where people met to do business and discuss events of the day. Many employers served a cup of tea to their workers in the middle of the morning, thus inventing a lasting British institution, the "tea break." However, drinking tea in social settings outside the workplace was beyond the means of the majority of British people. It came with a high price tag and tea was taxed as well.

Tea, the most typical English drink, became established in Britain because of the influence of a foreign princess, Catherine of Braganza, the queen of Charles II. A lover of tea since her childhood in Portugal, she brought tea-drinking to the English royal court and set a trend for the beverage in the seventeenth century. The fashion soon spread beyond the circle of the nobility to the middle classes, and tea became a popular drink at the London coffee houses where people met to do business and discuss events of the day. Many employers served a cup of tea to their workers in the middle of the morning, thus inventing a lasting British institution, the "tea break." However, drinking tea in social settings outside the workplace was beyond the means of the majority of British people. It came with a high price tag and tea was taxed as well.

Tea, the most typical English drink, became established in Britain because of the influence of a foreign princess, Catherine of Braganza, the queen of Charles II. A lover of tea since her childhood in Portugal, she brought tea-drinking to the English royal court and set a trend for the beverage in the seventeenth century. The fashion soon spread beyond the circle of the nobility to the middle classes, and tea became a popular drink at the London coffee houses where people met to do business and discuss events of the day. Many employers served a cup of tea to their workers in the middle of the morning , thus inventing a lasting British institution , the "tea break ." However, drinking tea in social settings outside the workplace was beyond the means of the majority of British people. It came with a high price tag and tea was taxed as well.

Tea, the most typical English drink, became established in Britain because of the influence of a foreign princess, Catherine of Braganza, the queen of Charles II. A lover of tea since her childhood in Portugal, she brought tea-drinking to the English royal court and set a trend for the beverage in the seventeenth century. The fashion soon spread beyond the circle of the nobility to the middle classes, and tea became a popular drink at the London coffee houses where people met to do business and discuss events of the day. Many employers served a cup of tea to their workers in the middle of the morning, thus inventing a lasting British institution, the "tea break." However , drinking tea in social settings outside the workplace was beyond the means of the majority of British people . It came with a high price tag and tea was taxed as well.

Tea, the most typical English drink, became established in Britain because of the influence of a foreign princess, Catherine of Braganza, the queen of Charles II. A lover of tea since her childhood in Portugal, she brought tea-drinking to the English royal court and set a trend for the beverage in the seventeenth century. The fashion soon spread beyond the circle of the nobility to the middle classes, and tea became a popular drink at the London coffee houses where people met to do business and discuss events of the day. Many employers served a cup of tea to their workers in the middle of the morning, thus inventing a lasting British institution, the "tea break." However, drinking tea in social settings outside the workplace was beyond the means of the majority of British people. It | came with | a high price tag | and | tea | was taxed | as well .

（第二段）

Around 1800 , the seventh Duchess of Bedford , Anne Maria , began the popular practice of "afternoon tea," a ceremony | taking place | at about four o'clock . Until then, people did not usually eat or drink anything between lunch and dinner. At approximately the same time, the Earl of Sandwich popularized a new way of eating bread—in thin slices, with something (e.g., jam or cucumbers) between them. Before long, a small meal at the end of the afternoon, involving tea and sandwiches, had become part of the British way of life.

Around 1800, the seventh Duchess of Bedford, Anne Maria, began the popular practice of "afternoon tea," a ceremony taking place at about four o'clock. Until then , people | did not usually | eat or drink | anything | between lunch and dinner . At approximately the same time, the Earl of Sandwich popularized a new way of eating bread—in thin slices, with something (e.g., jam or cucumbers) between them. Before long, a small meal at the end of the afternoon, involving tea and sandwiches, had become part of the British way of life.

Around 1800, the seventh Duchess of Bedford, Anne Maria, began the popular practice of "afternoon tea," a ceremony taking place at about four o'clock. Until then, people did not usually eat or drink anything between lunch and dinner. At approximately the same time , the Earl of Sandwich popularized a new way of eating bread —in thin slices , with something (e.g., jam or cucumbers) between them . Before long, a small meal at the end of the afternoon, involving tea and sandwiches, had become part of the British way of life.

Around 1800, the seventh Duchess of Bedford, Anne Maria, began the popular practice of "afternoon tea," a ceremony taking place at about four o'clock. Until then, people did not usually eat or drink anything between lunch and dinner. At approximately the same time, the Earl of Sandwich popularized a new way of eating bread—in thin slices, with something (e.g., jam or cucumbers) between them. Before long , a small meal at the end of the afternoon , involving tea and sandwiches , had become part of the British way of life .

（第三段）

As tea became much cheaper during the nineteenth century , its popularity spread right through all corners of the British society . Thus, tea became Britain's favorite drink. In working-class households, it was served with the main meal of the day, eaten when workers returned home after a day's labor. This meal has become known as "high tea."

As tea became much cheaper during the nineteenth century, its popularity spread right through all corners of the British society. Thus, tea became Britain's favorite drink . In working-class households, it was served with the main meal of the day, eaten when workers returned home after a day's labor. This meal has become known as "high tea."

As tea became much cheaper during the nineteenth century, its popularity spread right through all corners of the British society. Thus, tea became Britain's favorite drink. In working-class households , it was served with the main meal of the day , eaten when workers returned home after a day's labor . This meal has become known as "high tea."

As tea became much cheaper during the nineteenth century, its popularity spread right through all corners of the British society. Thus, tea became Britain's favorite drink. In working-class households, it was served with the main meal of the day, eaten when workers returned home after a day's labor. This meal has become known as " high tea ."

（第四段）

Today , tea can be drunk at any time of the day , and accounts for over two-fifths of all beverages consumed in Britain—with the exception of water.

Today, tea can be drunk at any time of the day, and accounts for over two-fifths of all beverages consumed in Britain — with the exception of water .

依據文意，請判斷對錯。若是對的就在括弧內打 O，錯就打 X。

不確定是否正確時，請勿回答或猜測答案

（未回答的題目請計算為錯誤題數）

❶ (　　)

Tea was expensive for most British people in the seventeenth century.

❷ (　　)

Around 1800, "afternoon tea" took place at three o'clock.

❸ (　　)

Tea became popular during the nineteenth century.

❹ (　　)

Nowadays, tea can be enjoyed at any time of the day.

❺ (　　)

Nowadays, tea accounts for one-fifths of all beverages consumed in Britain.

只花了 60 秒閱讀這篇文章，你答對了幾題？請對答案！

你的理解力＝(正確題數) 除以 5 再乘以 100%＝　　　　%

練習❸

〈單字〉

❶ marine

海中的 (adj.)

【例句】Dolphins are marine animals .

❷ fleeting

短暫的 (adj.)

【例句】At the end of July, he paid a fleeting visit to Taipei.

❸ lap up

舔食 (v.)

【例句】Her kittens have lapped up all the milk.

❹ dehydrated

脫水的 (adj.)

【例句】He loves dehydrated food such as dried mangoes.

❺ withered

乾枯的 (adj.)

【例句】There are some withered leaves on the ground.

請先花 5 秒鐘看看全文有多長即可 ⇨

練習❸

Many marine animals, including penguins and marine iguanas, have evolved ways to get rid of excess salt by using special salt-expelling glands around their tongue. However, the sea snake's salt glands cannot handle the massive amounts of salt that would enter their bodies if they actually drank seawater. This poses a serious problem when it comes to getting enough water to drink. If seawater is not an option, how does this animal survive in the ocean?

An international team of researchers focused on a population of yellow-bellied sea snakes living near Costa Rica, where rain often does not fall for up to seven months out of the year. Because yellow-bellied sea snakes usually spend all of their time far from land, rain is the animals' only source of fresh water. When it rains, a thin layer of fresh water forms on top of the ocean, providing the snakes with a fleeting opportunity to lap up that precious resource. But during the dry season when there is no rain, snakes presumably have nothing to drink. Thus, the team became interested in testing whether sea snakes became dehydrated at sea.

The researchers collected more than 500 yellow-bellied sea snakes and weighed them. They found that during the dry season about half of the snakes accepted fresh water offered to them, while nearly none did during the wet season. A snake's likelihood to drink also correlated with its body condition, with more withered snakes being more likely to drink, and to drink more. Finally, as predicted, snakes captured during the dry season contained significantly less body water than those scooped up in the rainy season. Thus, it seems the snake is able to endure certain degrees of dehydration in between rains. Scientists believe that dehydration at sea may explain the declining populations of sea snakes in some parts of the world.

（105年學測）

現在開始提升你的理解力吧！倒數計時 60 秒開始！

（第一段）

Many marine animals, including penguins and marine iguanas, have evolved ways to get rid of excess salt by using special salt-expelling glands around their tongue. However, the sea snake's salt glands cannot handle the massive amounts of salt that would enter their bodies if they actually drank seawater. This poses a serious problem when it comes to getting enough water to drink. If seawater is not an option, how does this animal survive in the ocean?

Many marine animals, including penguins and marine iguanas, have evolved ways to get rid of excess salt by using special salt-expelling glands around their tongue. However, the sea snake's salt glands cannot handle the massive amounts of salt that would enter their bodies if they actually drank seawater. This poses a serious problem when it comes to getting enough water to drink. If seawater is not an option, how does this animal survive in the ocean?

Many marine animals, including penguins and marine iguanas, have evolved ways to get rid of excess salt by using special salt-expelling glands around their tongue. However, the sea snake's salt glands cannot handle the massive amounts of salt that would enter their bodies if they actually drank seawater. This poses a serious problem when it comes to getting enough water to drink . If seawater is not an option , how does this animal survive in the ocean ?

（第二段）

An international team of researchers focused on a population of yellow-bellied sea snakes living near Costa Rica , where rain often does not fall for up to seven months out of the year . Because yellow-bellied sea snakes usually spend all of their time far from land, rain is the animals' only source of fresh water. When it rains, a thin layer of fresh water forms on top of the ocean, providing the snakes with a fleeting opportunity to lap up that precious resource. But during the dry season when there is no rain, snakes presumably have nothing to drink. Thus, the team became interested in testing whether sea snakes became dehydrated at sea.

An international team of researchers focused on a population of yellow-bellied sea snakes living near Costa Rica, where rain often does not fall for up to seven months out of the year. Because yellow-bellied sea snakes usually spend all of their time far from land , rain is the animals' only source of fresh water . When it rains, a thin layer of fresh water forms on top of the ocean, providing the snakes with a fleeting opportunity to lap up that precious resource. But during the dry season when there is no rain, snakes presumably have nothing to drink. Thus, the team became interested in testing whether sea snakes became dehydrated at sea.

An international team of researchers focused on a population of yellow-bellied sea snakes living near Costa Rica, where rain often does not fall for up to seven months out of the year. Because yellow-bellied sea snakes usually spend all of their time far from land, rain is the animals' only source of fresh water. When it rains, a thin layer of fresh water forms on top of the ocean, providing the snakes with a fleeting opportunity to lap up that precious resource. But during the dry season when there is no rain, snakes presumably have nothing to drink. Thus, the team became interested in testing whether sea snakes became dehydrated at sea.

An international team of researchers focused on a population of yellow-bellied sea snakes living near Costa Rica, where rain often does not fall for up to seven months out of the year. Because yellow-bellied sea snakes usually spend all of their time far from land, rain is the animals' only source of fresh water. When it rains, a thin layer of fresh water forms on top of the ocean, providing the snakes with a fleeting opportunity to lap up that precious resource. But during the dry season when there is no rain, snakes presumably have nothing to drink. Thus, the team became interested in testing whether sea snakes became dehydrated at sea.

（第三段）

The researchers collected more than 500 yellow-bellied sea snakes and weighed them. They found that during the dry season about half of the snakes accepted fresh water offered to them, while nearly none did during the wet season. A snake's likelihood to drink also correlated with its body condition, with more withered snakes being more likely to drink, and to drink more. Finally, as predicted, snakes captured during the dry season contained significantly less body water than those scooped up in the rainy season. Thus, it seems the snake is able to endure certain degrees of dehydration in between rains. Scientists believe that dehydration at sea may explain the declining populations of sea snakes in some parts of the world.

The researchers collected more than 500 yellow-bellied sea snakes and weighed them. They found that during the dry season about half of the snakes accepted fresh water offered to them, while nearly none did during the wet season. A snake's likelihood to drink also correlated with its body condition, with more withered snakes being more likely to drink, and to drink more. Finally, as predicted, snakes captured during the dry season contained significantly less body water than those scooped up in the rainy season. Thus, it seems the snake is able to endure certain degrees of dehydration in between rains. Scientists believe that dehydration at sea may explain the declining populations of sea snakes in some parts of the world.

The researchers collected more than 500 yellow-bellied sea snakes and weighed them. They found that during the dry season about half of the snakes accepted fresh water offered to them, while nearly none did during the wet season. A snake's likelihood to drink also correlated with its body condition, with more withered snakes being more likely to drink, and to drink more. Finally, as predicted, snakes captured during the dry season contained significantly less body water than those scooped up in the rainy season. Thus, it seems the snake is able to endure certain degrees of dehydration in between rains. Scientists believe that dehydration at sea may explain the declining populations of sea snakes in some parts of the world.

The researchers collected more than 500 yellow-bellied sea snakes and weighed them. They found that during the dry season about half of the snakes accepted fresh water offered to them, while nearly none did during the wet season. A snake's likelihood to drink also correlated with its body condition, with more withered snakes being more likely to drink, and to drink more. Finally , as predicted , snakes captured during the dry season contained significantly less body water than those scooped up in the rainy season . Thus, it seems the snake is able to endure certain degrees of dehydration in between rains. Scientists believe that dehydration at sea may explain the declining populations of sea snakes in some parts of the world.

The researchers collected more than 500 yellow-bellied sea snakes and weighed them. They found that during the dry season about half of the snakes accepted fresh water offered to them, while nearly none did during the wet season. A snake's likelihood to drink also correlated with its body condition, with more withered snakes being more likely to drink, and to drink more. Finally, as predicted, snakes captured during the dry season contained significantly less body water than those scooped up in the rainy season. Thus, it seems the snake is able to endure certain degrees of dehydration in between rains . Scientists believe that dehydration at sea may explain the declining populations of sea snakes in some parts of the world .

依據文意，請判斷對錯。若是對的就在括弧內打 O，錯就打 X。

不確定是否正確時，請勿回答或猜測答案

（未回答的題目請計算為錯誤題數）

❶ (　　)

Sea snakes can use salt-expelling glands around their tail.

❷ (　　)

The sea snake's salt glands can handle a lot of salt.

❸ (　　)

Sea snakes can drink fresh water that forms on top of the ocean.

❹ (　　)

In Costa Rica, rain may not fall for up to eleven months.

❺ (　　)

Snakes can endure a certain level of dehydration.

只花了 60 秒閱讀這篇文章，你答對了幾題？請對答案！

你的理解力＝(正確題數) 除以 5 再乘以 100% ＝ _____ ％

練習❹

〈單字〉

❶ myth
　傳聞 (n.)

　【例句】 I don't believe the myth that Jennifer is a worse driver than Mike.

❷ prose
　散文 (n.)

　【例句】 I like her unique prose style.

❸ racial discrimination
　種族歧視 (n.)

　【例句】 The school policy does not allow racial discrimination .

❹ an escape
　解脫 (n.)

　【例句】 He wanted an escape from his boring job.

❺ dust off
　重新拾起 (v.)

　【例句】 I am happy to dust off my old books and be a student again.

　　　　　請先花 5 秒鐘看看全文有多長即可　⇨

練習 ❹

American writer Toni Morrison was born in 1931 in Ohio. She was raised in an African American family filled with songs and stories of Southern myths, which later shaped her prose. Her happy family life led to her excellent performance in school, despite the atmosphere of racial discrimination in the society.

After graduating from college, Morrison started to work as a teacher and got married in 1958. Several years later, her marriage began to fail. For a temporary escape, she joined a small writers' group, in which each member was required to bring a story or poem for discussion. She wrote a story based on the life of a girl she knew in childhood who had prayed to God for blue eyes. The story was well received by the group, but then she put it away, thinking she was done with it.

In 1964, Morrison got divorced and devoted herself to writing. One day, she dusted off the story she had written for the writers' group and decided to make it into a novel. She drew on her memories from childhood and expanded upon them using her imagination so that the characters developed a life of their own. *The Bluest Eye* was eventually published in 1970. From 1970 to 1992, Morrison published five more novels.

In her novels, Morrison brings in different elements of the African American past, their struggles, problems and cultural memory. In *Song of Solomon*, for example, Morrison tells the story of an African American man and his search for identity in his culture. The novels and other works won her several prizes. In 1993, Morrison received the Nobel Prize in Literature. She is the eighth woman and the first African American woman to win the honor.

（103 年學測）

現在開始提升你的理解力吧！倒數計時 60 秒開始！

（第一段）

American writer Toni Morrison was born in 1931 in Ohio . She was raised in an African American family filled with songs and stories of Southern myths, which later shaped her prose. Her happy family life led to her excellent performance in school, despite the atmosphere of racial discrimination in the society.

American writer Toni Morrison was born in 1931 in Ohio. She was raised in an African American family filled with songs and stories of Southern myths , which later shaped her prose . Her happy family life led to her excellent performance in school, despite the atmosphere of racial discrimination in the society.

American writer Toni Morrison was born in 1931 in Ohio. She was raised in an African American family filled with songs and stories of Southern myths, which later shaped her prose. Her happy family life led to her excellent performance in school, despite the atmosphere of racial discrimination in the society.

（第二段）

After graduating | from college | , Morrison | started to work | as a teacher | and | got married | in 1958 . Several years later, her marriage began to fail . For a temporary escape, she joined a small writers' group, in which each member was required to bring a story or poem for discussion. She wrote a story based on the life of a girl she knew in childhood who had prayed to God for blue eyes. The story was well received by the group, but then she put it away, thinking she was done with it.

⇩

After graduating from college, Morrison started to work as a teacher and got married in 1958. Several years later , her marriage | began to fail . For a temporary escape, she joined a small writers' group, in which each member was required to bring a story or poem for discussion. She wrote a story based on the life of a girl she knew in childhood who had prayed to God for blue eyes. The story was well received by the group, but then she put it away, thinking she was done with it.

⇩

After graduating from college, Morrison started to work as a teacher and got married in 1958. Several years later, her marriage began to fail. For a temporary escape | , she | joined | a small writers' group | , in which | each member | was required to bring | a story or poem | for discussion . She wrote a story based on the life of a girl she knew in childhood who had prayed to God for blue eyes. The story was well received by the group, but then she put it away, thinking she was done with it.

⇩

After graduating from college, Morrison started to work as a teacher and got married in 1958. Several years later, her marriage began to fail. For a temporary escape, she joined a small writers' group, in which each member was required to bring a story or poem for discussion. She wrote a story based on the life of a girl she knew in childhood who had prayed to God for blue eyes. The story was well received by the group, but then she put it away, thinking she was done with it.

⇩

After graduating from college, Morrison started to work as a teacher and got married in 1958. Several years later, her marriage began to fail. For a temporary escape, she joined a small writers' group, in which each member was required to bring a story or poem for discussion. She wrote a story based on the life of a girl she knew in childhood who had prayed to God for blue eyes. The story was well received by the group, but then she put it away, thinking she was done with it.

（第三段）

In 1964, Morrison got divorced and devoted herself to writing. One day, she dusted off the story she had written for the writers' group and decided to make it into a novel. She drew on her memories from childhood and expanded upon them using her imagination so that the characters developed a life of their own. *The Bluest Eye* was eventually published in 1970. From 1970 to 1992, Morrison published five more novels.

⇩

In 1964, Morrison got divorced and devoted herself to writing. One day, she dusted off the story she had written for the writers' group and decided to make it into a novel. She drew on her memories from childhood and expanded upon them using her imagination so that the characters developed a life of their own. *The Bluest Eye* was eventually published in 1970. From 1970 to 1992, Morrison published five more novels.

⇩

In 1964, Morrison got divorced and devoted herself to writing. One day, she dusted off the story she had written for the writers' group and decided to make it into a novel. She drew on her memories from childhood and expanded upon them using her imagination so that the characters developed a life of their own. *The Bluest Eye* was eventually published in 1970. From 1970 to 1992, Morrison published five more novels.

⇩

In 1964, Morrison got divorced and devoted herself to writing. One day, she dusted off the story she had written for the writers' group and decided to make it into a novel. She drew on her memories from childhood and expanded upon them using her imagination so that the characters developed a life of their own. *The Bluest Eye* was eventually published in 1970. From 1970 to 1992, Morrison published five more novels.

（第四段）

In her novels , Morrison brings in different elements of the African American past , their struggles, problems and cultural memory . In *Song of Solomon*, for example, Morrison tells the story of an African American man and his search for identity in his culture. The novels and other works won her several prizes. In 1993, Morrison received the Nobel Prize in Literature. She is the eighth woman and the first African American woman to win the honor.

In her novels, Morrison brings in different elements of the African American past, their struggles, problems and cultural memory. In *Song of Solomon*, for example , Morrison tells the story of an African American man and his search for identity in his culture . The novels and other works won her several prizes. In 1993, Morrison received the Nobel Prize in Literature. She is the eighth woman and the first African American woman to win the honor.

In her novels, Morrison brings in different elements of the African American past, their struggles, problems and cultural memory. In *Song of Solomon*, for example, Morrison tells the story of an African American man and his search for identity in his culture. The novels and other works won her several prizes . In 1993, Morrison received the Nobel Prize in Literature. She is the eighth woman and the first African American woman to win the honor.

In her novels, Morrison brings in different elements of the African American past, their struggles, problems and cultural memory. In *Song of*

Solomon, for example, Morrison tells the story of an African American man and his search for identity in his culture. The novels and other works won her several prizes. In 1993 , Morrison received the Nobel Prize in Literature . She is the eighth woman and the first African American woman to win the honor.

In her novels, Morrison brings in different elements of the African American past, their struggles, problems and cultural memory. In *Song of Solomon*, for example, Morrison tells the story of an African American man and his search for identity in his culture. The novels and other works won her several prizes. In 1993, Morrison received the Nobel Prize in Literature. She is the eighth woman and the first African American woman to win the honor.

依據文意，請判斷對錯。若是對的就在括弧內打 O，錯就打 X。

不確定是否正確時，請勿回答或猜測答案

（未回答的題目請計算為錯誤題數）

❶ （ 　 ）

Morrison's marriage failed.

❷ （ 　 ）

Morrison was the first African American woman to win a Nobel Prize in Literature.

❸ （ 　 ）

Morrison published one novel.

❹ （ 　 ）

Morrison joined the writers' group in order to fight racial discrimination.

❺ （ 　 ）

This passage is mainly about the history of the Nobel Prize in Literature.

只花了 60 秒閱讀這篇文章，你答對了幾題？請對答案！

你的理解力＝(正確題數) 除以 5 再乘以 100%＝　　　　%

練習❺

〈單字〉

❶ Hindu religion
印度教 (n.)

【例句】 There are many followers of Hindu religion in Asia.

❷ dialect
方言 (n.)

【例句】 He didn't know many friends here because he did not
speak local dialects .

❸ hold
認為 (v.)

【例句】 Our tradition holds that red is a lucky color.

❹ piety
虔誠 (n.)

【例句】 They are followers of Hindu religion and are known for
their extreme piety.

請先花 5 秒鐘看看全文有多長即可 ⇨

練習❺

The majority of Indian women wear a red dot between their eyebrows. While it is generally taken as an indicator of their marital status, the practice is primarily related to the Hindu religion. The dot goes by different names in different Hindi dialects, and "bindi" is the one that is most commonly known. Traditionally, the dot carries no gender restriction: Men as well as women wear it. However, the tradition of men wearing it has faded in recent times, so nowadays we see a lot more women than men wearing one.

The position of the bindi is standard: center of the forehead, close to the eyebrows. It represents a third, or inner eye. Hindu tradition holds that all people have three eyes: The two outer ones are used for seeing the outside world, and the third one is there to focus inward toward God. As such, the dot signifies piety and serves as a constant reminder to keep God in the front of a believer's thoughts.

Red is the traditional color of the dot. It is said that in ancient times a man would place a drop of blood between his wife's eyes to seal their marriage. According to Hindu beliefs, the color red is believed to bring good fortune to the married couple. Today, people go with different colors depending upon their preferences. Women often wear dots that match the color of their clothes. Decorative or sticker bindis come in all sizes, colors and variations, and can be worn by young and old, married and unmarried people alike. Wearing a bindi has become more of a fashion statement than a religious custom.

（102 年學測）

現在開始提升你的理解力吧！倒數計時 60 秒開始！

（第一段）

The majority of Indian women │wear│ a red dot │between their eyebrows│. While it is generally taken as an indicator of their marital status, the practice is primarily related to the Hindu religion. The dot goes by different names in different Hindi dialects, and "bindi" is the one that is most commonly known. Traditionally, the dot carries no gender restriction: Men as well as women wear it. However, the tradition of men wearing it has faded in recent times, so nowadays we see a lot more women than men wearing one.

The majority of Indian women wear a red dot between their eyebrows. │While│ │it│ │is generally taken│ │as an indicator of│ │their marital status│, │the practice│ │is primarily related to│ │the Hindu religion│. The dot goes by different names in different Hindi dialects, and "bindi" is the one that is most commonly known. Traditionally, the dot carries no gender restriction: Men as well as women wear it. However, the tradition of men wearing it has faded in recent times, so nowadays we see a lot more women than men wearing one.

The majority of Indian women wear a red dot between their eyebrows. While it is generally taken as an indicator of their marital status, the practice is primarily related to the Hindu religion. │The dot│ │goes by different names│ │in different Hindi dialects│, │and│ "│bindi│"│is the one│ │that is most commonly known│. Traditionally, the dot carries no gender restriction: Men as well as women wear it. However, the tradition of men wearing it has faded in recent times, so nowadays we see a lot more women than men wearing one.

The majority of Indian women wear a red dot between their eyebrows. While it is generally taken as an indicator of their marital status, the practice is primarily related to the Hindu religion. The dot goes by different names in different Hindi dialects, and "bindi" is the one that is most commonly known. Traditionally, the dot carries no gender restriction: Men as well as women wear it. However, the tradition of men wearing it has faded in recent times, so nowadays we see a lot more women than men wearing one .

The majority of Indian women wear a red dot between their eyebrows. While it is generally taken as an indicator of their marital status, the practice is primarily related to the Hindu religion. The dot goes by different names in different Hindi dialects, and "bindi" is the one that is most commonly known. Traditionally, the dot carries no gender restriction: Men as well as women wear it. However, the tradition of men wearing it has faded in recent times, so nowadays we see a lot more women than men wearing one.

（第二段）

The position of the bindi is standard : center of the forehead, close to the eyebrows . It represents a third, or inner eye. Hindu tradition holds that all people have three eyes: The two outer ones are used for seeing the outside world, and the third one is there to focus inward toward God. As such, the dot signifies piety and serves as a constant reminder to keep God in the front of a believer's thoughts.

The position of the bindi is standard: center of the forehead, close to the eyebrows. |It| |represents| |a third, or inner eye|. |Hindu tradition| |holds that| |all people| |have| |three eyes|: The two outer ones are used for seeing the outside world, and the third one is there to focus inward toward God. As such, the dot signifies piety and serves as a constant reminder to keep God in the front of a believer's thoughts.

The position of the bindi is standard: center of the forehead, close to the eyebrows. It represents a third, or inner eye. Hindu tradition holds that all people have three eyes: |The two outer ones| |are used| |for seeing the outside world|, |and| |the third one| |is there to focus inward| |toward God|. As such, the dot signifies piety and serves as a constant reminder to keep God in the front of a believer's thoughts.

The position of the bindi is standard: center of the forehead, close to the eyebrows. It represents a third, or inner eye. Hindu tradition holds that all people have three eyes: The two outer ones are used for seeing the outside world, and the third one is there to focus inward toward God. As such, |the dot| |signifies| |piety| |and| |serves| |as a constant reminder| |to keep| |God| |in the front of| |a believer's thoughts|.

（第三段）

Red is the traditional color of the dot. It is said that in ancient times a man would place a drop of blood between his wife's eyes to seal their marriage. According to Hindu beliefs, the color red is believed to bring good fortune to the married couple. Today, people go with different colors depending upon their preferences. Women often wear dots that match the color of their clothes. Decorative or sticker bindis come in all sizes, colors and variations, and can be worn by young and old, married and unmarried people alike. Wearing a bindi has become more of a fashion statement than a religious custom.

Red is the traditional color of the dot. It is said that in ancient times a man would place a drop of blood between his wife's eyes to seal their marriage. According to Hindu beliefs, the color red is believed to bring good fortune to the married couple. Today, people go with different colors depending upon their preferences. Women often wear dots that match the color of their clothes. Decorative or sticker bindis come in all sizes, colors and variations, and can be worn by young and old, married and unmarried people alike. Wearing a bindi has become more of a fashion statement than a religious custom.

Red is the traditional color of the dot. It is said that in ancient times a man would place a drop of blood between his wife's eyes to seal their marriage. According to Hindu beliefs, the color red is believed to bring good fortune to the married couple. Today, people go with different colors depending upon their preferences. Women often wear dots that match the color of their clothes. Decorative or sticker bindis come in all sizes, colors and variations, and can be worn by young and old, married and unmarried people alike. Wearing a bindi has become more of a fashion statement than a religious custom.

Red is the traditional color of the dot. It is said that in ancient times a man would place a drop of blood between his wife's eyes to seal their marriage. According to Hindu beliefs, the color red is believed to bring good fortune to the married couple. Today, people go with different colors depending upon their preferences. Women often wear dots that match the color of their clothes. Decorative or sticker bindis come in all sizes, colors and variations, and can be worn by young and old, married and unmarried people alike. Wearing a bindi has become more of a fashion statement than a religious custom.

Red is the traditional color of the dot. It is said that in ancient times a man would place a drop of blood between his wife's eyes to seal their marriage. According to Hindu beliefs, the color red is believed to bring good fortune to the married couple. Today, people go with different colors depending upon their preferences. Women often wear dots that match the color of their clothes. Decorative or sticker bindis come in all sizes, colors and variations, and can be worn by young and old, married and unmarried people alike. Wearing a bindi has become more of a fashion statement than a religious custom.

Red is the traditional color of the dot. It is said that in ancient times a man would place a drop of blood between his wife's eyes to seal their marriage. According to Hindu beliefs, the color red is believed to bring good fortune to the married couple. Today, people go with different colors depending upon their preferences. Women often wear dots that match the color of their clothes. Decorative or sticker bindis come in all sizes, colors and variations, and can be worn by young and old, married and unmarried people alike. Wearing a bindi has become more of a fashion statement than a religious custom.

依據文意，請判斷對錯。若是對的就在括弧內打 O，錯就打 X。

不確定是否正確時，請勿回答或猜測答案

（未回答的題目請計算為錯誤題數）

❶ （　　）

The red dot that Indian women wear between their eyebrows has different names in different dialects.

❷ （　　）

The red dot represents a fourth eye.

❸ （　　）

Traditionally, men could also wear a red dot.

❹ （　　）

The color red protects married couples from danger.

❺ （　　）

Nowadays, both married and unmarried people in India can wear a dot between their eyebrows.

只花了 60 秒閱讀這篇文章，你答對了幾題？請對答案！

你的理解力＝(正確題數) 除以 5 再乘以 100% ＝ _____ %

練習❻

〈單字〉

❶ severe pain
劇痛 (n.)

【例句】 The patient is suffering from severe pain .

❷ mild
輕微的 (adj.)

【例句】 She is having a mild headache.

❸ intensity
強度 (n.)

【例句】 The scientists are trying to predict the intensity of the storm.

❹ cope with
面對 (v.)

【例句】 The book discusses ways to cope with stress.

請先花 5 秒鐘看看全文有多長即可 ⇨

練習❻

If you touch your finger to a hot stove, you know it's going to hurt. However, if you convince yourself beforehand that the pain won't be so bad, you might not suffer as much. According to a recent study, the part of your brain that reacts to severe pain is largely the same part that reacts to expectation of pain.

Researchers in this study worked with 10 volunteers, ages 24 to 46. Each volunteer wore a device that gave out 20-second-long pulses of heat to the right leg. There were three levels of heat, producing mild, moderate, or strong pain. During training, the volunteers would first hear a tone, followed by a period of silence, and then feel a heat pulse. They then learned to associate the length of the silent pause with the intensity of the upcoming heat pulse. The longer the pause, the stronger the heat pulse would be, causing more severe pain.

A day or two later, the real experiment began. The researchers found that the parts of the brain involved in learning, memory, emotion, and touch became more active as the volunteers expected higher levels of pain. These were mainly the same areas that became active when participants actually felt pain. Interestingly, when the volunteers expected only mild or moderate pain but experienced severe pain, they reported feeling 28 percent less pain than when they expected severe pain and actually got it.

The new study emphasizes that pain has both physical and psychological elements. Understanding how pain works in the mind and brain could eventually give doctors tools for helping people cope with painful medical treatments.

（97 年學測）

現在開始提升你的理解力吧！倒數計時 60 秒開始！

（第一段）

If you touch your finger to a hot stove , you know it's going to hurt . However, if you convince yourself beforehand that the pain won't be so bad, you might not suffer as much. According to a recent study, the part of your brain that reacts to severe pain is largely the same part that reacts to expectation of pain.

If you touch your finger to a hot stove, you know it's going to hurt. However , if you convince yourself beforehand that the pain won't be so bad , you might not suffer as much . According to a recent study, the part of your brain that reacts to severe pain is largely the same part that reacts to expectation of pain.

If you touch your finger to a hot stove, you know it's going to hurt. However, if you convince yourself beforehand that the pain won't be so bad, you might not suffer as much. According to a recent study , the part of your brain that reacts to severe pain is largely the same part that reacts to expectation of pain .

（第二段）

Researchers in this study worked with 10 volunteers , ages 24 to 46 .

Each volunteer | wore a device | that gave out | 20-second-long pulses | of heat | to the right leg |. There were three levels of heat, producing mild, moderate, or strong pain. During training, the volunteers would first hear a tone, followed by a period of silence, and then feel a heat pulse. They then learned to associate the length of the silent pause with the intensity of the upcoming heat pulse. The longer the pause, the stronger the heat pulse would be, causing more severe pain.

Researchers in this study worked with 10 volunteers, ages 24 to 46. Each volunteer wore a device that gave out 20-second-long pulses of heat to the right leg. There were | three levels of heat |, producing | mild, moderate, or strong pain |. During training |, the volunteers | would first hear | a tone |, followed by | a period of silence |, and then | feel | a heat pulse |. They then learned to associate the length of the silent pause with the intensity of the upcoming heat pulse. The longer the pause, the stronger the heat pulse would be, causing more severe pain.

Researchers in this study worked with 10 volunteers, ages 24 to 46. Each volunteer wore a device that gave out 20-second-long pulses of heat to the right leg. There were three levels of heat, producing mild, moderate, or strong pain. During training, the volunteers would first hear a tone, followed by a period of silence, and then feel a heat pulse. They | then | learned to associate | the length of the silent pause | with the intensity of | the upcoming heat pulse |. The longer the pause, the stronger the heat pulse would be, causing more severe pain.

Researchers in this study worked with 10 volunteers, ages 24 to 46. Each volunteer wore a device that gave out 20-second-long pulses of heat to the right leg. There were three levels of heat, producing mild, moderate, or strong pain. During training, the volunteers would first hear a tone, followed by a period of silence, and then feel a heat pulse. They then learned to associate the length of the silent pause with the intensity of the upcoming heat pulse. The longer the pause, the stronger the heat pulse would be, causing more severe pain.

（第三段）

A day or two later, the real experiment began. The researchers found that the parts of the brain involved in learning, memory, emotion, and touch became more active as the volunteers expected higher levels of pain. These were mainly the same areas that became active when participants actually felt pain. Interestingly, when the volunteers expected only mild or moderate pain but experienced severe pain, they reported feeling 28 percent less pain than when they expected severe pain and actually got it.

A day or two later, the real experiment began. The researchers found that the parts of the brain involved in learning, memory, emotion, and touch became more active as the volunteers expected higher levels of pain. These were mainly the same areas that became active when participants actually felt pain. Interestingly, when the volunteers expected only mild or moderate pain but experienced severe pain, they reported feeling 28 percent less pain than when they expected severe pain and actually got it.

A day or two later, the real experiment began. The researchers found that the parts of the brain involved in learning, memory, emotion, and touch became more active as the volunteers expected higher levels of pain. These were mainly the same areas that became active when participants actually felt pain . Interestingly, when the volunteers expected only mild or moderate pain but experienced severe pain, they reported feeling 28 percent less pain than when they expected severe pain and actually got it.

A day or two later, the real experiment began. The researchers found that the parts of the brain involved in learning, memory, emotion, and touch became more active as the volunteers expected higher levels of pain. These were mainly the same areas that became active when participants actually felt pain. Interestingly , when the volunteers expected only mild or moderate pain but experienced severe pain, they reported feeling 28 percent less pain than when they expected severe pain and actually got it.

（第四段）

The new study emphasizes that pain has both physical and psychological elements . Understanding how pain works in the mind and brain could eventually give doctors tools for helping people cope with painful medical treatments.

The new study emphasizes that pain has both physical and psychological elements. Understanding how pain works in the mind and brain could eventually give doctors tools for helping people cope with painful medical treatments .

依據文意，請判斷對錯。若是對的就在括弧內打 O，錯就打 X。
不確定是否正確時，請勿回答或猜測答案
（未回答的題目請計算為錯誤題數）

❶ （　　）

In the study, the heat pulses were given to the right arms of the volunteers.

❷ （　　）

Each heat pulse lasted for 20 seconds.

❸ （　　）

Pain only has physical elements.

❹ （　　）

There were three levels of heat.

❺ （　　）

The main idea of the passage is that patients should learn to be sensitive to pain.

只花了 60 秒閱讀這篇文章，你答對了幾題？請對答案！
你的理解力＝(正確題數) 除以 5 再乘以 100% ＝ _____ ％

練習❼

〈單字〉

❶ ancestor

先驅 (n.)

【例句】 Some people think that the traditional cell phone is the ancestor of the modern smartphone.

❷ hobby horse

兩輪舊式腳踏車 (n.)

【例句】 The hobby horse was invented 200 years ago.

❸ handlebar

腳踏車手把 (n.)

【例句】 When you ride a bicycle, you need to keep both of you hands on the handlebars .

❹ coach

四輪馬車 (n.)

【例句】 In the past, people travelled by coach pulled by horses.

❺ pedal

腳踏板 (n.)

【例句】 A bicycle usually has two pedals .

❻ collision

相撞 (n.)

【例句】 There was a collision between two cars this morning.

請先花 5 秒鐘看看全文有多長即可 ⇨

練習 ❼

Born in 1785 in southwestern Germany, Baron Karl Drais was one of the most creative German inventors of the 19th century. The Baron's numerous inventions include, among others, the earliest typewriter, the meat grinder, a device to record piano music on paper, and two four-wheeled human-powered vehicles. But it was the running machine, the modern ancestor of the bicycle, that made him famous.

The running machine, also called Draisine or hobby horse, was in effect a very primitive bicycle: it had no chains and was propelled by riders pushing off the ground with their feet. Though not a bike in the modern sense of the word, Drais' invention marked the big bang for the bicycle's development. It was the first vehicle with two wheels placed in line. The frame and wheels were made of wood; the steering already resembled a modern handlebar. Drais' big democratic idea behind his invention was to find a muscle-powered replacement for the horses, which were expensive and consumed lots of food even when not in use. The machine, he believed, would allow large numbers of people faster movement than walking or riding in a coach.

Drais undertook his first documented ride on June 12, 1817, covering a distance of 13 kilometers in one hour. A few months later, Drais created a huge sensation when he rode 60 kilometers in four hours. These were later followed by a marketing trip to Paris, where the hobby horse quickly caught on. The fad also quickly spread to Britain.

The success of the hobby horse was short-lived, though. They were heavy and difficult to ride. Safety was an issue, too: They lacked a brake, as well as cranks and pedals. There were frequent collisions with unsuspecting pedestrians, and after a few years Drais' invention was banned in many European and American cities. Drais' ideas, however, did not disappear entirely. Decades later, the machine was equipped by Frenchmen Pierre Lallement and Pierre Michaux with pedals to become the modern bicycle.

（107 年指考）

> 現在開始提升你的理解力吧！倒數計時 60 秒開始！

（第一段）

Born in 1785 | in southwestern Germany , Baron Karl Drais | was one of the most creative German inventors | of the 19th century . The Baron's numerous inventions include, among others, the earliest typewriter, the meat grinder, a device to record piano music on paper, and two four-wheeled human-powered vehicles. But it was the running machine, the modern ancestor of the bicycle, that made him famous.

Born in 1785 in southwestern Germany, Baron Karl Drais was one of the most creative German inventors of the 19th century. The Baron's numerous inventions | include , among others , the earliest typewriter , the meat grinder , a device to record piano music | on paper , and | two four-wheeled human-powered vehicles . But it was the running machine, the modern ancestor of the bicycle, that made him famous.

Born in 1785 in southwestern Germany, Baron Karl Drais was one of the most creative German inventors of the 19th century. The Baron's numerous inventions include, among others, the earliest typewriter, the meat grinder, a device to record piano music on paper, and two four-wheeled human-powered vehicles. But it was the running machine, the modern ancestor of the bicycle, that made him famous.

（第二段）

The running machine, also called Draisine or hobby horse, was in effect a very primitive bicycle : it had no chains and was propelled by riders pushing off the ground with their feet. Though not a bike in the modern sense of the word, Drais' invention marked the big bang for the bicycle's development. It was the first vehicle with two wheels placed in line. The frame and wheels were made of wood; the steering already resembled a modern handlebar. Drais' big democratic idea behind his invention was to find a muscle-powered replacement for the horses, which were expensive and consumed lots of food even when not in use. The machine, he believed, would allow large numbers of people faster movement than walking or riding in a coach.

The running machine, also called Draisine or hobby horse, was in effect a very primitive bicycle: it had no chains and was propelled by riders pushing off the ground with their feet. Though not a bike in the modern sense of the word, Drais' invention marked the big bang for the bicycle's development. It was the first vehicle with two wheels placed in line. The frame and wheels were made of wood; the steering already resembled a modern handlebar. Drais' big democratic idea behind his invention was to find a muscle-powered replacement for the horses, which were expensive and consumed lots of food even when not in use. The machine, he believed, would allow large numbers of people faster movement than walking or riding in a coach.

The running machine, also called Draisine or hobby horse, was in effect a very primitive bicycle: it had no chains and was propelled by riders pushing off the ground with their feet. Though not a bike in the modern sense of the word, Drais' invention marked the big bang for the bicycle's development. It was the first vehicle with two wheels placed in line. The frame and wheels were made of wood; the steering already resembled a modern handlebar. Drais' big democratic idea behind his invention was to find a muscle-powered replacement for the horses, which were expensive and consumed lots of food even when not in use. The machine, he believed, would allow large numbers of people faster movement than walking or riding in a coach.

The running machine, also called Draisine or hobby horse, was in effect a very primitive bicycle: it had no chains and was propelled by riders pushing off the ground with their feet. Though not a bike in the modern sense of the word, Drais' invention marked the big bang for the bicycle's development. It was the first vehicle with two wheels placed in line. The frame and wheels were made of wood; the steering already resembled a modern handlebar. Drais' big democratic idea behind his invention was to find a muscle-powered replacement for the horses, which were expensive and consumed lots of food even when not in use. The machine, he believed, would allow large numbers of people faster movement than walking or riding in a coach.

The running machine, also called Draisine or hobby horse, was in effect a very primitive bicycle: it had no chains and was propelled by riders pushing off the ground with their feet. Though not a bike in the modern sense of the word, Drais' invention marked the big bang for the bicycle's development. It was the first vehicle with two wheels placed in line. The frame and wheels were made of wood; the steering already resembled a modern handlebar. Drais' big democratic idea behind his invention was to find a muscle-powered replacement for the horses, which were expensive and consumed lots of food even when not in use. The machine, he believed, would allow large numbers of people faster movement than walking or riding in a coach.

The running machine, also called Draisine or hobby horse, was in effect a very primitive bicycle: it had no chains and was propelled by riders pushing off the ground with their feet. Though not a bike in the modern sense of the word, Drais' invention marked the big bang for the bicycle's development. It was the first vehicle with two wheels placed in line. The frame and wheels were made of wood; the steering already resembled a modern handlebar. Drais' big democratic idea behind his invention was to find a muscle-powered replacement for the horses, which were expensive and consumed lots of food even when not in use. The machine, he believed, would allow large numbers of people faster movement than walking or riding in a coach.

（第三段）

Drais undertook his first documented ride on June 12, 1817, covering a distance of 13 kilometers in one hour. A few months later, Drais created a huge sensation when he rode 60 kilometers in four hours. These were later followed by a marketing trip to Paris, where the hobby horse quickly caught on. The fad also quickly spread to Britain.

Drais undertook his first documented ride on June 12, 1817, covering a distance of 13 kilometers in one hour. A few months later, Drais created a huge sensation when he rode 60 kilometers in four hours. These were later followed by a marketing trip to Paris, where the hobby horse quickly caught on. The fad also quickly spread to Britain.

Drais undertook his first documented ride on June 12, 1817, covering a distance of 13 kilometers in one hour. A few months later, Drais created a huge sensation when he rode 60 kilometers in four hours. These were later followed by a marketing trip to Paris, where the hobby horse quickly caught on. The fad also quickly spread to Britain .

Drais undertook his first documented ride on June 12, 1817, covering a distance of 13 kilometers in one hour. A few months later, Drais created a huge sensation when he rode 60 kilometers in four hours. These were later followed by a marketing trip to Paris, where the hobby horse quickly caught on. The fad also quickly spread to Britain.

（第四段）

The success of the hobby horse was short-lived, though. They were heavy and difficult to ride. Safety was an issue, too: They lacked a brake, as well as cranks and pedals. There were frequent collisions with unsuspecting pedestrians, and after a few years Drais' invention was banned in many European and American cities. Drais' ideas, however, did not disappear entirely. Decades later, the machine was equipped by Frenchmen Pierre Lallement and Pierre Michaux with pedals to become the modern bicycle.

The success of the hobby horse was short-lived, though. They were heavy and difficult to ride. Safety was an issue, too: They lacked a brake, as well as cranks and pedals. There were frequent collisions with unsuspecting pedestrians, and after a few years Drais' invention was banned in many European and American cities. Drais' ideas, however, did not disappear entirely. Decades later, the machine was equipped by Frenchmen Pierre Lallement and Pierre Michaux with pedals to become the modern bicycle.

The success of the hobby horse was short-lived, though. They were heavy and difficult to ride. Safety was an issue, too: They lacked a brake, as well as cranks and pedals. There were frequent collisions with unsuspecting pedestrians, and after a few years Drais' invention was banned in many European and American cities. Drais' ideas, however, did not disappear entirely. Decades later, the machine was equipped by Frenchmen Pierre Lallement and Pierre Michaux with pedals to become the modern bicycle.

⇩

The success of the hobby horse was short-lived, though. They were heavy and difficult to ride. Safety was an issue, too: They lacked a brake, as well as cranks and pedals. There were | frequent collisions | with unsuspecting pedestrians |, and | after a few years | Drais' invention | was banned | in many European and American cities . Drais' ideas, however, did not disappear entirely. Decades later, the machine was equipped by Frenchmen Pierre Lallement and Pierre Michaux with pedals to become the modern bicycle.

⇩

The success of the hobby horse was short-lived, though. They were heavy and difficult to ride. Safety was an issue, too: They lacked a brake, as well as cranks and pedals. There were frequent collisions with unsuspecting pedestrians, and after a few years Drais' invention was banned in many European and American cities. Drais' ideas |, however |, did not disappear | entirely . Decades later, the machine was equipped by Frenchmen Pierre Lallement and Pierre Michaux with pedals to become the modern bicycle.

⇩

The success of the hobby horse was short-lived, though. They were heavy and difficult to ride. Safety was an issue, too: They lacked a brake, as well as cranks and pedals. There were frequent collisions with unsuspecting pedestrians, and after a few years Drais' invention was banned in many European and American cities. Drais' ideas, however, did not disappear entirely. Decades later |, the machine | was equipped | by Frenchmen Pierre Lallement and Pierre Michaux | with pedals | to become | the modern bicycle .

依據文意，請判斷對錯。若是對的就在括弧內打 O，錯就打 X。

不確定是否正確時，請勿回答或猜測答案

（未回答的題目請計算為錯誤題數）

❶ （　　）

The running machine was also called hobby horse.

❷ （　　）

The wheels of the running machine were made of wood.

❸ （　　）

The running machine had a brake to control the speed.

❹ （　　）

The running machine became common in the 19th century.

❺ （　　）

The running machine was easy to ride.

只花了 60 秒閱讀這篇文章，你答對了幾題？請對答案！

你的理解力＝(正確題數) 除以 5 再乘以 100%＝ ＿＿＿ %

練習❽

〈單字〉

❶ forensic linguistics

司法語言學 (n.)

【例句】 Forensic linguistics is different from traditional linguistics.

❷ intersect

交疊 (v.)

【例句】 Educational linguistics is a research field where education and linguistics intersect.

❸ graffiti

塗鴉 (n.)

【例句】 Graffiti in New York City has been considered as a form of street art.

❹ resort to

求助於 (v.)

【例句】 In order to run his business, he resorted to another loan from his parents.

❺ prominence

成名 (n.)

【例句】 Michael Jordan quickly gained prominence in the NBA.

❻ casualties

傷亡 (n.)

【例句】 The army suffered high casualties in the war.

請先花 5 秒鐘看看全文有多長即可

練習❽

The term "forensic linguistics," in its broadest sense, covers all areas of study where language and law intersect. A famous example of its application is the case of Chris Coleman, who was suspected of killing his family in 2009. Robert Leonard, the head of the forensic linguistics program at Hofstra University, presented some important linguistic evidence in the trial against Coleman. Relying heavily on word choice and spelling, Leonard suggested that the same person had written the threatening e-mails and sprayed the graffiti, and that those samples bore similarities to Coleman's writing style. Coleman was later found guilty of the murder.

Robert Leonard was not the first one who resorted to linguistic evidence in criminal investigation. The field of forensic linguistics was brought to prominence by his colleague James Fitzgerald in 1996 with his work in the case of the Unabomber, who had sent a series of letter bombs to college professors over several years, causing serious casualties. Working for the FBI, Fitzgerald urged the publication of the Unabomber's letter—a lengthy declaration of the criminal's philosophy.

After the letter was published, many people called the FBI to say they recognized the writing style. By analyzing sentence structure, word choice, and other linguistic patterns, Fitzgerald narrowed down the range of possible authors and finally linked the letter to the writings of Ted Kaczynski, a solitary former mathematician. For instance, Kaczynski tended to use extensive parallel phrases, which were frequently found in the bomber's letter. Both Kaczynski and the bomber also showed a preference for dozens of unusual words, such as "chimerical" and "anomic." The bomber's use of the terms "broad" for women and "negro" for African Americans also enabled Fitzgerald to roughly calculate the suspect's age. The linguistic evidence was strong enough for the judge to search Kaczynski's isolated cabin in Montana; what was found there put him in prison for life.

On some level, finding hidden meanings from linguistic evidence is what we all do intuitively in our daily language interaction. This is exactly the same work forensic professionals do. As one forensic-linguistics firm, Testipro, puts it in its online promotional ad, the field can be regarded as "the basis of the entire legal system."

（106 年學測）

> 現在開始提升你的理解力吧！請翻到次頁，倒數計時 60 秒開始！

（第一段）

The term "forensic linguistics," in its broadest sense, covers all areas of study where language and law intersect. A famous example of its application is the case of Chris Coleman, who was suspected of killing his family in 2009. Robert Leonard, the head of the forensic linguistics program at Hofstra University, presented some important linguistic evidence in the trial against Coleman. Relying heavily on word choice and spelling, Leonard suggested that the same person had written the threatening e-mails and sprayed the graffiti, and that those samples bore similarities to Coleman's writing style. Coleman was later found guilty of the murder.

The term "forensic linguistics," in its broadest sense, covers all areas of study where language and law intersect. A famous example of its application is the case of Chris Coleman, who was suspected of killing his family in 2009. Robert Leonard, the head of the forensic linguistics program at Hofstra University, presented some important linguistic evidence in the trial against Coleman. Relying heavily on word choice and spelling, Leonard suggested that the same person had written the threatening e-mails and sprayed the graffiti, and that those samples bore similarities to Coleman's writing style. Coleman was later found guilty of the murder.

The term "forensic linguistics," in its broadest sense, covers all areas of study where language and law intersect. A famous example of its application is the case of Chris Coleman, who was suspected of killing his family in 2009. Robert Leonard, the head of the forensic linguistics program at

Hofstra University , presented some important linguistic evidence in the trial against Coleman . Relying heavily on word choice and spelling, Leonard suggested that the same person had written the threatening e-mails and sprayed the graffiti, and that those samples bore similarities to Coleman's writing style. Coleman was later found guilty of the murder.

The term "forensic linguistics," in its broadest sense, covers all areas of study where language and law intersect. A famous example of its application is the case of Chris Coleman, who was suspected of killing his family in 2009. Robert Leonard, the head of the forensic linguistics program at Hofstra University, presented some important linguistic evidence in the trial against Coleman. Relying heavily on word choice and spelling , Leonard suggested that the same person had written the threatening e-mails and sprayed the graffiti , and that those samples bore similarities to Coleman's writing style . Coleman was later found guilty of the murder .

The term "forensic linguistics," in its broadest sense, covers all areas of study where language and law intersect. A famous example of its application is the case of Chris Coleman, who was suspected of killing his family in 2009. Robert Leonard, the head of the forensic linguistics program at Hofstra University, presented some important linguistic evidence in the trial against Coleman. Relying heavily on word choice and spelling, Leonard suggested that the same person had written the threatening e-mails and sprayed the graffiti, and that those samples bore similarities to Coleman's writing style. Coleman was later found guilty of the murder .

（第二段）

Robert Leonard was not the first one who resorted to linguistic evidence in criminal investigation. The field of forensic linguistics was brought to prominence by his colleague James Fitzgerald in 1996 with his work in the case of the Unabomber, who had sent a series of letter bombs to college professors over several years, causing serious casualties. Working for the FBI, Fitzgerald urged the publication of the Unabomber's letter—a lengthy declaration of the criminal's philosophy.

Robert Leonard was not the first one who resorted to linguistic evidence in criminal investigation. The field of forensic linguistics was brought to prominence by his colleague James Fitzgerald in 1996 with his work in the case of the Unabomber, who had sent a series of letter bombs to college professors over several years, causing serious casualties. Working for the FBI, Fitzgerald urged the publication of the Unabomber's letter—a lengthy declaration of the criminal's philosophy.

Robert Leonard was not the first one who resorted to linguistic evidence in criminal investigation. The field of forensic linguistics was brought to prominence by his colleague James Fitzgerald in 1996 with his work in the case of the Unabomber, who had sent a series of letter bombs to college professors over several years, causing serious casualties. Working for the FBI, Fitzgerald urged the publication of the Unabomber's letter—a lengthy declaration of the criminal's philosophy.

（第三段）

After | the letter | was published |, | many people | called the FBI | to say |
they | recognized | the writing style |. By analyzing sentence structure, word choice, and other linguistic patterns, Fitzgerald narrowed down the range of possible authors and finally linked the letter to the writings of Ted Kaczynski, a solitary former mathematician. For instance, Kaczynski tended to use extensive parallel phrases, which were frequently found in the bomber's letter. Both Kaczynski and the bomber also showed a preference for dozens of unusual words, such as "chimerical" and "anomic." The bomber's use of the terms "broad" for women and "negro" for African Americans also enabled Fitzgerald to roughly calculate the suspect's age. The linguistic evidence was strong enough for the judge to search Kaczynski's isolated cabin in Montana; what was found there put him in prison for life.

After the letter was published, many people called the FBI to say they recognized the writing style. | By analyzing | sentence structure, word choice, and other linguistic patterns |, | Fitzgerald | narrowed down | the range of | possible authors | and | finally linked | the letter | to the writings of Ted Kaczynski |, | a solitary former mathematician |. For instance, Kaczynski tended to use extensive parallel phrases, which were frequently found in the bomber's letter. Both Kaczynski and the bomber also showed a preference for dozens of unusual words, such as "chimerical" and "anomic." The bomber's use of the terms "broad" for women and "negro" for African Americans also enabled Fitzgerald to roughly calculate the suspect's age. The linguistic evidence was strong enough for the judge to search Kaczynski's isolated cabin in Montana; what was found there put him in prison for life.

After the letter was published, many people called the FBI to say they recognized the writing style. By analyzing sentence structure, word choice, and other linguistic patterns, Fitzgerald narrowed down the range of possible authors and finally linked the letter to the writings of Ted Kaczynski, a solitary former mathematician. For instance, Kaczynski tended to use extensive parallel phrases, which were frequently found in the bomber's letter. Both Kaczynski and the bomber also showed a preference for dozens of unusual words, such as "chimerical" and "anomic." The bomber's use of the terms "broad" for women and "negro" for African Americans also enabled Fitzgerald to roughly calculate the suspect's age. The linguistic evidence was strong enough for the judge to search Kaczynski's isolated cabin in Montana; what was found there put him in prison for life.

After the letter was published, many people called the FBI to say they recognized the writing style. By analyzing sentence structure, word choice, and other linguistic patterns, Fitzgerald narrowed down the range of possible authors and finally linked the letter to the writings of Ted Kaczynski, a solitary former mathematician. For instance, Kaczynski tended to use extensive parallel phrases, which were frequently found in the bomber's letter. Both Kaczynski and the bomber also showed a preference for dozens of unusual words, such as "chimerical" and "anomic." The bomber's use of the terms "broad" for women and "negro" for African Americans also enabled Fitzgerald to roughly calculate the suspect's age. The linguistic evidence was strong enough for the judge to search Kaczynski's isolated cabin in Montana; what was found there put him in prison for life.

After the letter was published, many people called the FBI to say they recognized the writing style. By analyzing sentence structure, word choice, and other linguistic patterns, Fitzgerald narrowed down the range of possible authors and finally linked the letter to the writings of Ted Kaczynski, a solitary former mathematician. For instance, Kaczynski tended to use extensive parallel phrases, which were frequently found in the bomber's letter. Both Kaczynski and the bomber also showed a preference for dozens of unusual words, such as "chimerical" and "anomic." The bomber's use of the terms "broad" for women and "negro" for African Americans also enabled Fitzgerald to roughly calculate the suspect's age. The linguistic evidence was strong enough for the judge to search Kaczynski's isolated cabin in Montana; what was found there put him in prison for life.

After the letter was published, many people called the FBI to say they recognized the writing style. By analyzing sentence structure, word choice, and other linguistic patterns, Fitzgerald narrowed down the range of possible authors and finally linked the letter to the writings of Ted Kaczynski, a solitary former mathematician. For instance, Kaczynski tended to use extensive parallel phrases, which were frequently found in the bomber's letter. Both Kaczynski and the bomber also showed a preference for dozens of unusual words, such as "chimerical" and "anomic." The bomber's use of the terms "broad" for women and "negro" for African Americans also enabled Fitzgerald to roughly calculate the suspect's age. The linguistic evidence was strong enough for the judge to search Kaczynski's isolated cabin in Montana; what was found there put him in prison for life.

（第四段）

On some level , finding hidden meanings from linguistic evidence is what we all do intuitively in our daily language interaction . This is exactly the same work forensic professionals do. As one forensic-linguistics firm, *Testipro*, puts it in its online promotional ad, the field can be regarded as "the basis of the entire legal system."

On some level, finding hidden meanings from linguistic evidence is what we all do intuitively in our daily language interaction. This is exactly the same work forensic professionals do . As one forensic-linguistics firm, *Testipro*, puts it in its online promotional ad, the field can be regarded as "the basis of the entire legal system."

On some level, finding hidden meanings from linguistic evidence is what we all do intuitively in our daily language interaction. This is exactly the same work forensic professionals do. As one forensic-linguistics firm , *Testipro*, puts it in its online promotional ad , the field can be regarded as "the basis of the entire legal system. "

依據文意，請判斷對錯。若是對的就在括弧內打 O，錯就打 X。

不確定是否正確時，請勿回答或猜測答案

（未回答的題目請計算為錯誤題數）

❶ (　　)

Forensic linguistics relies on word choice, spelling, sentence structures, and other linguistic patterns.

❷ (　　)

People tend to use similar linguistic patterns in their use of language.

❸ (　　)

FBI failed to use linguistic evidence in criminal investigation.

❹ (　　)

Many people were able to recognize the writing style of the Unabomber.

❺ (　　)

The main idea of the passage is that finding hidden meanings in language use is important for our daily interactions.

只花了 60 秒閱讀這篇文章，你答對了幾題？請對答案！

你的理解力 =(正確題數) 除以 5 再乘以 100% = ＿＿＿＿%

練習❾

❶ ethnic group
種族 (n.)

【例句】 There are different ethnic groups in the United States.

❷ spear
用矛刺 (v.)

【例句】 He speared fish in the river,

❸ garment
服裝 (n.)

【例句】 Winter garments are on sale today.

❹ due to
因為

【例句】 Her success is due to her hard work.

❺ aggressive
有攻擊性的 (adj.)

【例句】 The boy is looking at the aggressive dog.

請先花 5 秒鐘看看全文有多長即可 ⇨

練習 ❾

It is easy for us to tell our friends from our enemies. But can other animals do the same? Elephants can! They can use their sense of vision and smell to tell the difference between people who pose a threat and those who do not.

In Kenya, researchers found that elephants react differently to clothing worn by men of the Maasai and Kamba ethnic groups. Young Maasai men spear animals and thus pose a threat to elephants; Kamba men are mainly farmers and are not a danger to elephants.

In an experiment conducted by animal scientists, elephants were first presented with clean clothing or clothing that had been worn for five days by either a Maasai or a Kamba man. When the elephants detected the smell of clothing worn by a Maasai man, they moved away from the smell faster and took longer to relax than when they detected the smells of either clothing worn by Kamba men or clothing that had not been worn at all.

Garment color also plays a role, though in a different way. In the same study, when the elephants saw red clothing not worn before, they reacted angrily, as red is typically worn by Maasai men. Rather than running away as they did with the smell, the elephants acted aggressively toward the red clothing.

The researchers believe that the elephants' emotional reactions are due to their different interpretations of the smells and the sights. Smelling a potential danger means that a threat is nearby and the best thing to do is run away and hide. Seeing a potential threat without its smell means that risk is low. Therefore, instead of showing fear and running away, the elephants express their anger and become aggressive.

（100 年學測）

現在開始提升你的理解力吧！倒數計時 60 秒開始！

（第一段）

It is easy | for us | to tell our friends | from our enemies . But | can | other animals | do the same ? Elephants can ! They can use their sense of vision and smell to tell the difference between people who pose a threat and those who do not.

⇩

It is easy for us to tell our friends from our enemies. But can other animals do the same? Elephants can! They | can use | their sense of | vision and smell | to tell the difference | between people who pose a threat | and | those who do not .

（第二段）

In Kenya , researchers | found that | elephants | react differently to clothing worn by men of | the Maasai and Kamba ethnic groups . Young Maasai men spear animals and thus pose a threat to elephants; Kamba men are mainly farmers and are not a danger to elephants.

⇩

In Kenya, researchers found that elephants react differently to clothing worn by men of the Maasai and Kamba ethnic groups. Young Maasai men | spear | animals | and thus pose | a threat | to elephants ; Kamba men | are mainly farmers | and | are not a danger to elephants .

（第三段）

In an experiment | conducted by | animal scientists ,| elephants | were first presented with | clean clothing | or | clothing that had been worn | for five days | by either a Maasai | or a Kamba man . When the elephants detected the smell of clothing worn by a Maasai man, they moved away from the smell faster and took longer to relax than when they detected the smells of either clothing worn by Kamba men or clothing that had not been worn at all.

In an experiment conducted by animal scientists, elephants were first presented with clean clothing or clothing that had been worn for five days by either a Maasai or a Kamba man. When the elephants | detected | the smell of clothing | worn by a Maasai man ,| they | moved away | from the smell | faster and | took longer to relax | than when they | detected | the smells of | either clothing | worn by Kamba men | or clothing | that had not been worn | at all .

（第四段）

Garment color | also plays a role ,| though | in a different way .| In the same study ,| when the elephants | saw | red clothing | not worn before ,| they | reacted angrily ,| as red | is typically worn by | Maasai men . Rather than running away as they did with the smell, the elephants acted aggressively toward the red clothing.

Garment color also plays a role, though in a different way. In the same study, when the elephants saw red clothing not worn before, they reacted angrily, as red is typically worn by Maasai men. Rather than running away as they did with the smell, the elephants acted aggressively toward the red clothing.

（第五段）

The researchers believe that the elephants' emotional reactions are due to their different interpretations of the smells and the sights. Smelling a potential danger means that a threat is nearby and the best thing to do is run away and hide. Seeing a potential threat without its smell means that risk is low. Therefore, instead of showing fear and running away, the elephants express their anger and become aggressive.

The researchers believe that the elephants' emotional reactions are due to their different interpretations of the smells and the sights. Smelling a potential danger means that a threat is nearby and the best thing to do is run away and hide. Seeing a potential threat without its smell means that risk is low. Therefore, instead of showing fear and running away, the elephants express their anger and become aggressive.

The researchers believe that the elephants' emotional reactions are due to their different interpretations of the smells and the sights. Smelling a potential danger means that a threat is nearby and the best thing to do is run away and hide. Seeing a potential threat without its smell means that risk is low. Therefore, instead of showing fear and running away, the elephants express their anger and become aggressive.

The researchers believe that the elephants' emotional reactions are due to their different interpretations of the smells and the sights. Smelling a potential danger means that a threat is nearby and the best thing to do is run away and hide. Seeing a potential threat without its smell means that risk is low. Therefore, instead of showing fear and running away, the elephants express their anger and become aggressive.

依據文意，請判斷對錯。若是對的就在括弧內打 O，錯就打 X。

不確定是否正確時，請勿回答或猜測答案

（未回答的題目請計算為錯誤題數）

❶ (　　)

Maasai people are a threat to elephants.

❷ (　　)

Maasai people typically wear yellow clothing.

❸ (　　)

In this study, elephants attacked a man with the smell of new clothing.

❹ (　　)

In this study, elephants ran away when they smelled Maasai people.

❺ (　　)

Elephants use sight and smell to detect danger.

只花了 60 秒閱讀這篇文章，你答對了幾題？請對答案！

你的理解力＝(正確題數) 除以 5 再乘以 100% ＝ ＿＿＿ %

練習❿

〈單字〉

❶ forge

建立 (v.)

【例句】They have $\boxed{\text{forged}}$ a friendly relationship.

❷ antagonize

激怒 (v.)

【例句】She $\boxed{\text{antagonized}}$ her friend this afternoon.

❸ tension

對立 (n.)

【例句】There was some $\boxed{\text{tension}}$ in the meeting.

❹ put-down

嘲笑人的話 (n.)

【例句】Mike dislikes her $\boxed{\text{put-downs}}$.

❺ take a toll

造成傷害 (v.)

【例句】You need to relax because stress will $\boxed{\text{take a toll}}$ on you.

❻ erode

傷害 (v.)

【例句】Her failure on the exam $\boxed{\text{eroded}}$ her confidence.

請先花 5 秒鐘看看全文有多長即可

練習 ⑩

A sense of humor is something highly valued. A person who has a great sense of humor is often considered to be happy and socially confident. However, humor is a double-edged sword. It can forge better relationships and help you cope with life, but sometimes it can also damage self-esteem and antagonize others.

People who use bonding humor tell jokes and generally lighten the mood. They're perceived as being good at reducing the tension in uncomfortable situations. They often make fun of their common experiences, and sometimes they may even laugh off their own misfortunes. The basic message they deliver is: We're all alike, we find the same things funny, and we're all in this together.

Put-down humor, on the other hand, is an aggressive type of humor used to criticize and manipulate others through teasing. When it's aimed against politicians, as it often is, it's hilarious and mostly harmless. But in the real world, it may have a harmful impact. An example of such humor is telling friends an embarrassing story about another friend. When challenged about their teasing, the put-down jokers might claim that they are "just kidding," thus allowing themselves to avoid responsibility. This type of humor, though considered by some people to be socially acceptable, may hurt the feelings of the one being teased and thus take a toll on personal relationships.

Finally, in hate-me humor, the joker is the target of the joke for the amusement of others. This type of humor was used by comedians John Belushi and Chris Farley—both of whom suffered for their success in show business. A small dose of such humor is charming, but routinely offering oneself up to be humiliated erodes one's self-respect, and fosters depression and anxiety.

So it seems that being funny isn't necessarily an indicator of good social skills and well-being. In certain cases, it may actually have a negative impact on interpersonal relationships.

（101 年指考）

現在開始提升你的理解力吧！倒數計時 60 秒開始！

（第一段）

A sense of humor is something highly valued. A person who has a great sense of humor is often considered to be happy and socially confident. However, humor is a double-edged sword. It can forge better relationships and help you cope with life, but sometimes it can also damage self-esteem and antagonize others.

A sense of humor is something highly valued. A person who has a great sense of humor is often considered to be happy and socially confident. However, humor is a double-edged sword. It can forge better relationships and help you cope with life, but sometimes it can also damage self-esteem and antagonize others.

A sense of humor is something highly valued. A person who has a great sense of humor is often considered to be happy and socially confident. However, humor is a double-edged sword. It can forge better relationships and help you cope with life, but sometimes it can also damage self-esteem and antagonize others.

A sense of humor is something highly valued. A person who has a great sense of humor is often considered to be happy and socially confident. However, humor is a double-edged sword. It can forge better relationships and help you cope with life, but sometimes it can also damage self-esteem and antagonize others.

（第二段）

People who use bonding humor tell jokes and generally lighten the mood. They're perceived as being good at reducing the tension in uncomfortable situations. They often make fun of their common experiences, and sometimes they may even laugh off their own misfortunes. The basic message they deliver is: We're all alike, we find the same things funny, and we're all in this together.

People who use bonding humor tell jokes and generally lighten the mood. They're perceived as being good at reducing the tension in uncomfortable situations. They often make fun of their common experiences, and sometimes they may even laugh off their own misfortunes. The basic message they deliver is: We're all alike, we find the same things funny, and we're all in this together.

People who use bonding humor tell jokes and generally lighten the mood. They're perceived as being good at reducing the tension in uncomfortable situations. They often make fun of their common experiences, and sometimes they may even laugh off their own misfortunes. The basic message they deliver is: We're all alike, we find the same things funny, and we're all in this together.

People who use bonding humor tell jokes and generally lighten the mood. They're perceived as being good at reducing the tension in uncomfortable situations. They often make fun of their common experiences, and sometimes they may even laugh off their own misfortunes. The basic message they deliver is: We're all alike, we find the same things funny, and we're all in this together.

（第三段）

Put-down humor, on the other hand, is an aggressive type of humor used to criticize and manipulate others through teasing. When it's aimed against politicians, as it often is, it's hilarious and mostly harmless. But in the real world, it may have a harmful impact. An example of such humor is telling friends an embarrassing story about another friend. When challenged about their teasing, the put-down jokers might claim that they are "just kidding," thus allowing themselves to avoid responsibility. This type of humor, though considered by some people to be socially acceptable, may hurt the feelings of the one being teased and thus take a toll on personal relationships.

Put-down humor, on the other hand, is an aggressive type of humor used to criticize and manipulate others through teasing. When it's aimed against politicians, as it often is, it's hilarious and mostly harmless. But in the real world, it may have a harmful impact. An example of such humor is telling friends an embarrassing story about another friend. When challenged about their teasing, the put-down jokers might claim that they are "just kidding," thus allowing themselves to avoid responsibility. This type of humor, though considered by some people to be socially acceptable, may hurt the feelings of the one being teased and thus take a toll on personal relationships.

Put-down humor, on the other hand, is an aggressive type of humor used to criticize and manipulate others through teasing. When it's aimed against politicians, as it often is, it's hilarious and mostly harmless. But in the real world, it may have a harmful impact. An example of such humor is telling friends an embarrassing story about another friend. When challenged about their teasing, the put-down jokers might claim that they are "just kidding," thus allowing themselves to avoid responsibility. This type of humor, though considered by some people to be socially acceptable, may hurt the feelings of the one being teased and thus take a toll on personal relationships.

Put-down humor, on the other hand, is an aggressive type of humor used to criticize and manipulate others through teasing. When it's aimed against politicians, as it often is, it's hilarious and mostly harmless. But in the real world, it may have a harmful impact. An example of such humor is telling friends an embarrassing story about another friend. When challenged about their teasing, the put-down jokers might claim that they are "just kidding," thus allowing themselves to avoid responsibility. This type of humor, though considered by some people to be socially acceptable, may hurt the feelings of the one being teased and thus take a toll on personal relationships.

Put-down humor, on the other hand, is an aggressive type of humor used to criticize and manipulate others through teasing. When it's aimed against politicians, as it often is, it's hilarious and mostly harmless. But in the real world, it may have a harmful impact. An example of such humor is telling friends an embarrassing story about another friend. When challenged about their teasing, the put-down jokers might claim that they are "just kidding," thus allowing themselves to avoid responsibility. This type of humor, though considered by some people to be socially acceptable, may hurt the feelings of the one being teased and thus take a toll on personal relationships.

Put-down humor, on the other hand, is an aggressive type of humor used to criticize and manipulate others through teasing. When it's aimed against politicians, as it often is, it's hilarious and mostly harmless. But in the real world, it may have a harmful impact. An example of such humor is telling friends an embarrassing story about another friend. When challenged about their teasing, the put-down jokers might claim that they are "just kidding," thus allowing themselves to avoid responsibility. This type of humor, though considered by some people to be socially acceptable, may hurt the feelings of | the one being teased | and thus | take a toll on | personal relationships .

（第四段）

Finally , in hate-me humor , the joker | is the target of the joke | for the amusement of others . This type of humor was used by comedians John Belushi and Chris Farley—both of whom suffered for their success in show business. A small dose of such humor is charming, but routinely offering oneself up to be humiliated erodes one's self-respect, and fosters depression and anxiety.

Finally, in hate-me humor, the joker is the target of the joke for the amusement of others. This type of humor | was used by | comedians John Belushi and Chris Farley | —both of whom | suffered for | their success | in show business . A small dose of such humor is charming, but routinely offering oneself up to be humiliated erodes one's self-respect, and fosters depression and anxiety.

Finally, in hate-me humor, the joker is the target of the joke for the amusement of others. This type of humor was used by comedians John Belushi and Chris Farley—both of whom suffered for their success in show business. A small dose of | such humor | is charming , but | routinely offering | oneself | up to be humiliated | erodes | one's self-respect , and | fosters | depression and anxiety .

（第五段）

So | it seems that | being funny | isn't necessarily an indicator of | good social skills and well-being . In certain cases, it may actually have a negative impact on interpersonal relationships.

So it seems that being funny isn't necessarily an indicator of good social skills and well-being. In certain cases , it | may actually have | a negative impact on | interpersonal relationships .

依據文意，請判斷對錯。若是對的就在括弧內打 O，錯就打 X。

不確定是否正確時，請勿回答或猜測答案

（未回答的題目請計算為錯誤題數）

❶ (　　)

Politicians are common targets of put-down humor.

❷ (　　)

Put-down humor is used to criticize others.

❸ (　　)

Both John Belushi and Chris Farley used put-down humor.

❹ (　　)

Bonding humor creates a relaxing atmosphere by joking about experiences that people all have.

❺ (　　)

Humor has both its bright side and dark side.

只花了 60 秒閱讀這篇文章，你答對了幾題？請對答案！

你的理解力＝(正確題數) 除以 5 再乘以 100% =　　　　%

第六堂課

實戰練習（二）

練習❶

〈單字〉

❶ martial art
   武術 (n.)
   【例句】Karate is a martial art .

❷ acrobatics
   雜技 (n.)
   【例句】 Acrobatics is very difficult.

❸ slavery
   奴役 (n.)
   【例句】 Slavery no longer exists in the United States.

❹ camouflage
   偽裝 (v.)
   【例句】 Some lizards camouflage themselves by changing colors.

請先花 5 秒鐘看看全文有多長即可 ⇨

練習❶

Capoeira is a martial art that combines elements of fight, acrobatics, drumming, singing, dance, and rituals. It involves a variety of techniques that make use of the hands, feet, legs, arms, and head. Although Capoeira appears dancelike, many of its basic techniques are similar to those in other martial arts.

Capoeira was created nearly 500 years ago in Brazil by African slaves. It is believed that the martial art was connected with tribal fighting in Africa, in which people fought body to body, without weapons, in order to acquire a bride or desired woman. In the sixteenth century, when the Africans were taken from their homes to Brazil against their will and kept in slavery, Capoeira began to take form among the community of slaves for self-defense. But it soon became a strong weapon in the life-or-death struggle against their oppressors. When the slave owners realized the power of Capoeira, they began to punish those who practiced it. Capoeiristas learned to camouflage the forbidden fights with singing, clapping, and dancing as though it were simply entertainment.

At first, Capoeira was considered illegal in Brazil. However, a man known as Mestre Bimba devoted a great deal of time and effort to convincing the Brazilian authorities that Capoeira has great cultural value and should become an official fighting style. He succeeded in his endeavor and transformed the martial art into Brazil's national sport. He and Mestre Pastinha were the first to open schools, and the Capoeira tree grew, spreading its branches across the world. Nowadays, it is performed in movies and music clips. Capoeira is also believed to have influenced several dancing styles like breaking and hip-hop.

（106 年學測）

現在開始提升你的理解力吧！倒數計時 60 秒開始！

（第一段）

Capoeira is a martial art that combines elements of fight, acrobatics, drumming, singing, dance, and rituals . It involves a variety of techniques that make use of the hands, feet, legs, arms, and head . Although Capoeira appears dancelike, many of its basic techniques are similar to those in other martial arts.

Capoeira is a martial art that combines elements of fight, acrobatics, drumming, singing, dance, and rituals. It involves a variety of techniques that make use of the hands, feet, legs, arms, and head. Although Capoeira appears dancelike, many of its basic techniques are similar to those in other martial arts .

（第二段）

Capoeira was created nearly 500 years ago in Brazil by African slaves . It is believed that the martial art was connected with tribal fighting in Africa , in which people fought body to body , without weapons , in order to acquire a bride or desired woman . In the sixteenth century, when the Africans were taken from their homes to Brazil against their will and kept in slavery, Capoeira began to take form among the community of slaves for self-defense. But it soon became a strong weapon in the life-or-death struggle against their oppressors. When the slave owners realized the power of Capoeira, they began to punish those who practiced it. Capoeiristas learned to camouflage the forbidden fights with singing, clapping, and dancing as though it were simply entertainment.

Capoeira was created nearly 500 years ago in Brazil by African slaves. It is believed that the martial art was connected with tribal fighting in Africa, in which people fought body to body, without weapons, in order to acquire a bride or desired woman. In the sixteenth century , when the Africans were taken from their homes to Brazil against their will and kept in slavery , Capoeira began to take form among the community of slaves for self-defense . But it soon became a strong weapon in the life-or-death struggle against their oppressors. When the slave owners realized the power of Capoeira, they began to punish those who practiced it. Capoeiristas learned to camouflage the forbidden fights with singing, clapping, and dancing as though it were simply entertainment.

Capoeira was created nearly 500 years ago in Brazil by African slaves. It is believed that the martial art was connected with tribal fighting in Africa, in which people fought body to body, without weapons, in order to acquire a bride or desired woman. In the sixteenth century, when the Africans were taken from their homes to Brazil against their will and kept in slavery, Capoeira began to take form among the community of slaves for self-defense. But it soon became a strong weapon in the life-or-death struggle against their oppressors. When the slave owners realized the power of Capoeira, they began to punish those who practiced it. Capoeiristas learned to camouflage the forbidden fights with singing, clapping, and dancing as though it were simply entertainment.

（第三段）

At first, Capoeira was considered illegal in Brazil. However, a man known as Mestre Bimba devoted a great deal of time and effort to convincing the Brazilian authorities that Capoeira has great cultural value and should become an official fighting style. He succeeded in his endeavor and transformed the martial art into Brazil's national sport. He and Mestre Pastinha were the first to open schools, and the Capoeira tree grew, spreading its branches across the world. Nowadays, it is performed in movies and music clips. Capoeira is also believed to have influenced several dancing styles like breaking and hip-hop.

At first, Capoeira was considered illegal in Brazil. However, a man known as Mestre Bimba devoted a great deal of time and effort to convincing the Brazilian authorities that Capoeira has great cultural value and should become an official fighting style. He succeeded in his endeavor and transformed the martial art into Brazil's national sport. He and Mestre Pastinha were the first to open schools, and the Capoeira tree grew, spreading its branches across the world. Nowadays, it is performed in movies and music clips. Capoeira is also believed to have influenced several dancing styles like breaking and hip-hop.

At first, Capoeira was considered illegal in Brazil. However, a man known as Mestre Bimba devoted a great deal of time and effort to convincing the Brazilian authorities that Capoeira has great cultural value and should become an official fighting style. He succeeded in his endeavor and transformed the martial art into Brazil's national sport. He and Mestre Pastinha were the first to open schools, and the Capoeira tree grew, spreading its branches across the world. Nowadays, it is performed in movies and music clips. Capoeira is also believed to have influenced several dancing styles like breaking and hip-hop.

依據文意，請判斷對錯。若是對的就在括弧內打 O，錯就打 X。

不確定是否正確時，請勿回答或猜測答案

（未回答的題目請計算為錯誤題數）

❶ (　　　)

Capoeira looks like dancing.

❷ (　　　)

Capoeira was created by American slaves.

❸ (　　　)

The slave owners punished those who practiced Capoeira.

❹ (　　　)

Mestre Bimba made Capoeira illegal in Brazil.

❺ (　　　)

This passage is mainly about the techniques of Capoeira.

只花了 60 秒閱讀這篇文章，你答對了幾題？請對答案！

你的理解力＝(正確題數) 除以 5 再乘以 100% ＝ ＿＿＿＿ %

練習❷

〈單字〉

❶ massive

大規模的 (adj.)

【例句】 There has been a massive increase in the number of seeking financial assistance.

❷ artificial intelligence

人工智慧 (n.)

【例句】 Artificial intelligence has been a popular area of research.

❸ cash-strapped

有經濟困難的 (adj.)

【例句】 The cash-strapped school is trying to get more students.

❹ hard drive

硬碟 (n.)

【例句】 New computers often come with hard drives that can store a lot of data.

請先花 5 秒鐘看看全文有多長即可 ⇨

練習❷

MOOC, a massive open online course, aims at providing large-scale interactive participation and open access via the web. In addition to traditional course materials such as videos, readings, and problem sets, MOOCs provide interactive user forums that help build a community for the students, professors, and teaching assistants.

MOOCs first made waves in the fall of 2011, when Professor Sebastian Thrun from Stanford University opened his graduate-level artificial intelligence course up to any student anywhere, and 160,000 students in more than 190 countries signed up. This new breed of online classes is shaking up the higher education world in many ways. Since the courses can be taken by hundreds of thousands of students at the same time, the number of universities might decrease dramatically. Professor Thrun has even envisioned a future in which there will only need to be 10 universities in the world. Perhaps the most striking thing about MOOCs, many of which are being taught by professors at prestigious universities, is that they're free. This is certainly good news for cash-strapped students.

There is a lot of excitement and fear surrounding MOOCs. While some say free online courses are a great way to increase the enrollment of minority students, others have said they will leave many students behind. Some critics have said that MOOCs promote an unrealistic one-size-fits-all model of higher education and that there is no replacement for true dialogues between professors and their students. After all, a brain is not a computer. We are not blank hard drives waiting to be filled with data. People learn from people they love and remember the things that arouse emotion. Some critics worry that online students will miss out on the social aspects of college. （103 年學測）

現在開始提升你的理解力吧！倒數計時 60 秒開始！

（第一段）

MOOC, a massive open online course , aims at providing large-scale interactive participation and open access via the web . In addition to traditional course materials such as videos, readings , and problem sets , MOOCs provide interactive user forums that help build a community for the students, professors, and teaching assistants .

（第二段）

MOOCs first made waves in the fall of 2011 , when Professor Sebastian Thrun from Stanford University opened his graduate-level artificial intelligence course up to any student anywhere , and 160,000 students in more than 190 countries signed up . This new breed of online classes is shaking up the higher education world in many ways . Since the courses can be taken by hundreds of thousands of students at the same time, the number of universities might decrease dramatically. Professor Thrun has even envisioned a future in which there will only need to be 10 universities in the world. Perhaps the most striking thing about MOOCs, many of which are being taught by professors at prestigious universities, is that they're free. This is certainly good news for cash-strapped students.

MOOCs first made waves in the fall of 2011, when Professor Sebastian Thrun from Stanford University opened his graduate-level artificial intelligence course up to any student anywhere, and 160,000 students in more than 190 countries signed up. This new breed of online classes is shaking up the higher education world in many ways. Since the courses can be taken by hundreds of thousands of students at the same time, the number of universities might decrease dramatically. Professor Thrun has even envisioned a future in which there will only need to be 10 universities in the world. Perhaps the most striking thing about MOOCs, many of which are being taught by professors at prestigious universities, is that they're free. This is certainly good news for cash-strapped students.

MOOCs first made waves in the fall of 2011, when Professor Sebastian Thrun from Stanford University opened his graduate-level artificial intelligence course up to any student anywhere, and 160,000 students in more than 190 countries signed up. This new breed of online classes is shaking up the higher education world in many ways. Since the courses can be taken by hundreds of thousands of students at the same time, the number of universities might decrease dramatically. Professor Thrun has even envisioned a future in which there will only need to be 10 universities in the world. Perhaps the most striking thing about MOOCs, many of which are being taught by professors at prestigious universities, is that they're free. This is certainly good news for cash-strapped students.

（第三段）

There is | a lot of excitement and fear | surrounding | MOOCs . While some | say | free online courses | are a great way | to increase | the enrollment of minority students , others | have said | they | will leave | many students behind . Some critics have said that MOOCs promote an unrealistic one-size-fits-all model of higher education and that there is no replacement for true dialogues between professors and their students. After all, a brain is not a computer. We are not blank hard drives waiting to be filled with data. People learn from people they love and remember the things that arouse emotion. Some critics worry that online students will miss out on the social aspects of college.

There is a lot of excitement and fear surrounding MOOCs. While some say free online courses are a great way to increase the enrollment of minority students, others have said they will leave many students behind. Some critics have said that | MOOCs | promote | an unrealistic one-size-fits-all model of higher education | and that | there is | no replacement for | true dialogues between professors and their students . After all , a brain | is not a computer . We | are not blank hard drives | waiting to be filled | with data . People | learn from | people they love | and | remember | the things | that arouse | emotion . Some critics | worry that | online students | will miss out on | the social aspects of college .

依據文意，請判斷對錯。若是對的就在括弧內打 O，錯就打 X。

不確定是否正確時，請勿回答或猜測答案

（未回答的題目請計算為錯誤題數）

❶ （　　）

MOOCs' tuition fees <u>are high</u>.

❷ （　　）

MOOCs are suitable for students <u>who are short of money</u>.

❸ （　　）

Many students can take the course <u>at the same time</u>.

❹ （　　）

MOOCs <u>can replace</u> dialogues between professors and their students.

❺ （　　）

One of the problems of MOOCs is <u>the lack of social interaction</u>.

只花了 60 秒閱讀這篇文章，你答對了幾題？請對答案！

你的理解力＝(正確題數) 除以 5 再乘以 100%＝ ＿＿＿ %

練習❸

〈單字〉

❶ Babylonian

　　巴比倫人 (n.)（巴比倫王國是四千多年前「四大文明古國」之一）

　　【例句】 Babylonians lived in a city located in Western Asia.

❷ lullaby

　　搖籃催眠曲 (n.)

　　【例句】 A lullaby is a song used to make children go to sleep.

❸ sleeping-inducing

　　令人想睡的 (adj.)

　　【例句】 The song is really sleep-inducing .

❹ scold

　　責罵 (v.)

　　【例句】 She scolded her children for not doing their homework.

❺ undertone

　　含意 (n.)

　　【例句】 There is an undertone of sadness in his email.

> 請先花 5 秒鐘看看全文有多長即可　⇨

練習❸

Four millennia ago, an ancient Babylonian wrote down what is possibly the first lullaby. It is a rather threatening lullaby, in which the baby is scolded for disturbing the house god with its crying and warned of terrifying consequences. It may have got the baby to sleep, but its message is far from comforting: If he/she does not stop crying, the demon will eat him/her. This lullaby may sound more scary than sleep-inducing, yet it is true that many lullabies—including those sung today—have dark undertones.

Research has shown that lullabies, when used correctly, can soothe and possibly even help to heal an infant; but it is the caretaker's voice and the rhythm and melody of the music that babies respond to, not the content of the song. Then, what is the function of the content? According to studies, some lullabies provide advice, like the Babylonian lullaby, and quite a few others offer the space to sing the unsung, say the unsayable. Lyrics to those lullabies can indeed be interpreted as a reflection of the caregiver's emotions.

Researchers believe that a large part of the function of lullabies is to help a mother vocalize her worries and concerns. The mother's fear of loss especially makes sense since the infant/toddler years of life are fragile ones. Since there is a special physical bond between mother and child during this period, mothers feel they can sing to their child about their own fears and anxieties. Lullabies, therefore, serve as therapy for the mother. In addition, the songs are seemingly trying to work some magic—as if, by singing, the mother is saying, "Sadness has already touched this house; no need to come by again."　（107 年學測）

現在開始提升你的理解力吧！請翻到次頁，倒數計時 60 秒開始！

（第一段）

Four millennia ago , an ancient Babylonian wrote down what is possibly the first lullaby . It is a rather threatening lullaby , in which the baby is scolded for disturbing the house god with its crying and warned of terrifying consequences . It may have got the baby to sleep, but its message is far from comforting: If he/she does not stop crying, the demon will eat him/her. This lullaby may sound more scary than sleep-inducing, yet it is true that many lullabies—including those sung today—have dark undertones.

⇩

Four millennia ago, an ancient Babylonian wrote down what is possibly the first lullaby. It is a rather threatening lullaby, in which the baby is scolded for disturbing the house god with its crying and warned of terrifying consequences. It may have got the baby to sleep , but its message is far from comforting : If he/she does not stop crying , the demon will eat him/her . This lullaby may sound more scary than sleep-inducing , yet it is true that many lullabies — including those sung today — have dark undertones .

（第二段）

Research has shown that lullabies , when used correctly , can soothe and possibly even help to heal an infant ; but it is the caretaker's voice and the rhythm and melody of the music that babies respond to , not the content of the song . Then , what is the function of the content ? According to studies, some lullabies provide advice, like the Babylonian lullaby, and quite a few others offer the space to sing the unsung, say the unsayable. Lyrics to those lullabies can indeed be interpreted as a reflection of the caregiver's emotions.

Research has shown that lullabies, when used correctly, can soothe and possibly even help to heal an infant; but it is the caretaker's voice and the rhythm and melody of the music that babies respond to, not the content of the song. Then, what is the function of the content? According to studies, some lullabies provide advice, like the Babylonian lullaby, and quite a few others offer the space to sing the unsung, say the unsayable. Lyrics to those lullabies can indeed be interpreted as a reflection of the caregiver's emotions.

（第三段）

Researchers believe that a large part of the function of lullabies is to help a mother vocalize her worries and concerns. The mother's fear of loss especially makes sense since the infant/toddler years of life are fragile ones. Since there is a special physical bond between mother and child during this period, mothers feel they can sing to their child about their own fears and anxieties. Lullabies, therefore, serve as therapy for the mother. In addition, the songs are seemingly trying to work some magic—as if, by singing, the mother is saying, "Sadness has already touched this house; no need to come by again."

Researchers believe that a large part of the function of lullabies is to help a mother vocalize her worries and concerns. The mother's fear of loss especially makes sense since the infant/toddler years of life are fragile ones. Since there is a special physical bond between mother and child during this period, mothers feel they can sing to their child about their own fears and anxieties. Lullabies, therefore, serve as therapy for the mother. In addition, the songs are seemingly trying to work some magic — as if, by singing, the mother is saying, "Sadness has already touched this house; no need to come by again."

依據文意，請判斷對錯。若是對的就在括弧內打 O，錯就打 X。

不確定是否正確時，請勿回答或猜測答案

（未回答的題目請計算為錯誤題數）

❶ (   )

What is possibly the first lullaby is threatening.

❷ (   )

Many lullabies that we sing today are comforting.

❸ (   )

Lullabies comfort not only the baby but also the mother.

❹ (   )

One of the functions of lullabies is to help mothers express their worries.

❺ (   )

Babies react to the content of lullabies.

只花了 60 秒閱讀這篇文章，你答對了幾題？請對答案！

你的理解力 =(正確題數) 除以 5 再乘以 100% = ＿＿＿ %

練習❹

〈單字〉

❶ vast

巨大的 (adj.)

【例句】The professor has a vast amount of scientific knowledge.

❷ authorities

主管機關 (n.)

【例句】Local authorities are very concerned with this car accident.

❸ figure

數字 (n.)

【例句】U.S. unemployment figures have dropped recently.

❹ alternative

替代方案 (n.)

【例句】 He cannot come today, but tomorrow is an alternative .

❺ measure

政策措施 (n.)

【例句】 He suggested some measures to reduce traffic accidents.

請先花 5 秒鐘看看全文有多長即可　⇨

In an ideal world, people would not test medicines on animals. Such experiments are stressful and sometimes painful for animals, and expensive and time-consuming for people. Yet animal experimentation is still needed to help bridge vast gaps in medical knowledge. That is why there are some 50 to 100 million animals used in research around the world each year.

Europe, on the whole, has the world's most restrictive laws on animal experiments. Even so, its scientists use some 12 million animals a year, most of them mice and rats, for medical research. Official statistics show that just 1.1 million animals are used in research in America each year. But that is misleading. The American authorities do not think mice and rats are worth counting and, as these are the most common laboratory animals, the true figure is much higher. Japan and China have even less comprehensive data than America.

Now Europe is reforming the rules governing animal experiments by restricting the number of animals used in labs. Alternatives to animal testing, such as using human tissue or computer models, are now strongly recommended. In addition, sharing all research results freely should help to reduce the number of animals for scientific use. At present, scientists often share only the results of successful experiments. If their findings do not fit the hypothesis being tested, the work never sees the light of day. This practice means wasting time, money, and animals' lives in endlessly repeating the failed experiments.

Animal experimentation has taught humanity a great deal and saved countless lives. It needs to continue, even if that means animals sometimes suffer. Europe's new measures should eventually both reduce the number of animals used in experiments and improve the way in which scientific research is conducted.

（100 年指考）

現在開始提升你的理解力吧！倒數計時 60 秒開始！

（第一段）

In an ideal world , people would not test medicines on animals . Such experiments are stressful and sometimes painful for animals , and expensive and time-consuming for people . Yet animal experimentation is still needed to help bridge vast gaps in medical knowledge . That is why there are some 50 to 100 million animals used in research around the world each year .

（第二段）

Europe , on the whole , has the world's most restrictive laws on animal experiments . Even so , its scientists use some 12 million animals a year , most of them mice and rats , for medical research . Official statistics show that just 1.1 million animals are used in research in America each year. But that is misleading. The American authorities do not think mice and rats are worth counting and, as these are the most common laboratory animals, the true figure is much higher. Japan and China have even less comprehensive data than America.

Europe, on the whole, has the world's most restrictive laws on animal experiments. Even so, its scientists use some 12 million animals a year, most of them mice and rats, for medical research. Official statistics show that just 1.1 million animals are used in research in America each year . But that is misleading . The American authorities do not think mice and rats are worth counting and , as these are the most common laboratory animals , the true figure is much higher . Japan and China have even less comprehensive data than America .

（第三段）

Now Europe is reforming the rules governing animal experiments by restricting the number of animals used in labs . Alternatives to animal testing , such as using human tissue or computer models , are now strongly recommended . In addition, sharing all research results freely should help to reduce the number of animals for scientific use. At present, scientists often share only the results of successful experiments. If their findings do not fit the hypothesis being tested, the work never sees the light of day. This practice means wasting time, money, and animals' lives in endlessly repeating the failed experiments.

Now Europe is reforming the rules governing animal experiments by restricting the number of animals used in labs. Alternatives to animal testing, such as using human tissue or computer models, are now strongly recommended. In addition , sharing all research results freely should help to reduce the number of animals for scientific use . At present , scientists often share only the results of successful experiments . If their findings do not fit the hypothesis being tested, the work never sees the light of day. This practice means wasting time, money, and animals' lives in endlessly repeating the failed experiments.

Now Europe is reforming the rules governing animal experiments by restricting the number of animals used in labs. Alternatives to animal testing, such as using human tissue or computer models, are now strongly recommended. In addition, sharing all research results freely should help to reduce the number of animals for scientific use. At present, scientists often share only the results of successful experiments. If their findings do not fit the hypothesis being tested , the work never sees the light of day . This practice means wasting time, money, and animals' lives in endlessly repeating the failed experiments .

（第四段）

Animal experimentation has taught humanity a great deal and saved countless lives . It needs to continue , even if that means animals sometimes suffer . Europe's new measures should eventually both reduce the number of animals used in experiments and improve the way in which scientific research is conducted.

Animal experimentation has taught humanity a great deal and saved countless lives. It needs to continue, even if that means animals sometimes suffer. Europe's new measures should eventually both reduce the number of animals used in experiments and improve the way in which scientific research is conducted .

依據文意，請判斷對錯。若是對的就在括弧內打 O，錯就打 X。
不確定是否正確時，請勿回答或猜測答案
（未回答的題目請計算為錯誤題數）

❶ (　　)

America has the world's most restrictive laws on animal experiments.

❷ (　　)

Computer models are an alternative to animal experiments.

❸ (　　)

Unsuccessful animal experiments are not revealed to the public.

❹ (　　)

Japan and China have more comprehensive data than America.

❺ (　　)

The main idea of this passage is that scientists should share their research results with each other.

只花了 60 秒閱讀這篇文章，你答對了幾題？請對答案！
你的理解力＝(正確題數) 除以 5 再乘以 100% ＝ _____ ％

練習❺

〈單字〉

❶ carve

雕刻 (v.)

【例句】She carved her name into the wall.

❷ edge

邊緣 (n.)

【例句】He put his book on the edge of the table.

❸ motto

座右銘 (n.)

【例句】'Never give up' is her motto .

❹ inscription

刻印的文字 (n.)

【例句】 He saw an inscription on the wall.

❺ deceased

過世的 (adj.)

【例句】 He was a student of the recently deceased scientist Stephen Hawking.

請先花 5 秒鐘看看全文有多長即可 ⇨

練習❺

　　The following report appeared in a newspaper in February 2007. On February 15, 2007, hundreds of people came to New York City's famous railroad station—Grand Central Terminal—to trade in old dollar bills for the new George Washington presidential US $1 coins. The gold-colored coin is the first in a new series by the U.S. Mint to honor former U.S. presidents. The Mint will issue four presidential US $1 coins a year through 2016. These coins will come out in the order in which each president served. The George Washington coin is the first to be released. John Adams, Thomas Jefferson and James Madison coins will come out later this year.

　　The presidential US $1 coins have a special design. For the first time since the 1930s, there are words carved into the edge of each coin, including the year in which the coin was issued and traditional mottos. Each coin will show a different president on its face, or heads side. It will also show the president's name. The other side of the coin will show the Statue of Liberty and the inscriptions "United States of America" and "$1."

　　There are some interesting facts about the coins. First, there will be one presidential US $1 coin for each president, except Grover Cleveland. He will have two! Cleveland is the only U.S. president to have served two nonconsecutive terms. The last president now scheduled to get a coin is Gerald Ford. That's because a president cannot appear on a coin when he is still alive. In addition, a president must have been deceased for two years before he can be on a coin.

（99 年指考）

現在開始提升你的理解力吧！倒數計時 60 秒開始！

（第一段）

The following report appeared in a newspaper in February 2007. On February 15, 2007, hundreds of people came to New York City's famous railroad station—Grand Central Terminal—to trade in old dollar bills for the new George Washington presidential US $1 coins. The gold-colored coin is the first in a new series by the U.S. Mint to honor former U.S. presidents. The Mint will issue four presidential US $1 coins a year through 2016. These coins will come out in the order in which each president served. The George Washington coin is the first to be released. John Adams, Thomas Jefferson and James Madison coins will come out later this year.

The following report appeared in a newspaper in February 2007. On February 15, 2007, hundreds of people came to New York City's famous railroad station—Grand Central Terminal—to trade in old dollar bills for the new George Washington presidential US $1 coins. The gold-colored coin is the first in a new series by the U.S. Mint to honor former U.S. presidents. The Mint will issue four presidential US $1 coins a year through 2016. These coins will come out in the order in which each president served. The George Washington coin is the first to be released. John Adams, Thomas Jefferson and James Madison coins will come out later this year.

The following report appeared in a newspaper in February 2007. On February 15, 2007, hundreds of people came to New York City's famous railroad station—Grand Central Terminal—to trade in old dollar bills for the new George Washington presidential US $1 coins. The gold-colored coin is the first in a new series by the U.S. Mint to honor former U.S. presidents. The Mint will issue four presidential US $1 coins a year through 2016. These coins will come out in the order in which each president served . The George Washington coin is the first to be released . John Adams, Thomas Jefferson and James Madison coins will come out later this year .

（第二段）

The presidential US $1 coins have a special design . For the first time since the 1930s , there are words carved into the edge of each coin , including the year in which the coin was issued and traditional mottos . Each coin will show a different president on its face, or heads side. It will also show the president's name. The other side of the coin will show the Statue of Liberty and the inscriptions "United States of America" and "$1."

The presidential US $1 coins have a special design. For the first time since the 1930s, there are words carved into the edge of each coin, including the year in which the coin was issued and traditional mottos. Each coin will show a different president on its face , or heads side . It will also show the president's name . The other side of the coin will show the Statue of Liberty and the inscriptions "United States of America" and "$1."

The presidential US $1 coins have a special design. For the first time since the 1930s, there are words carved into the edge of each coin, including the year in which the coin was issued and traditional mottos. Each coin will show a different president on its face, or heads side. It will also show the president's name. The other side of the coin | will show | the Statue of Liberty | and | the inscriptions | "United States of America" | and | " | $1 | ."

（第三段）

There are | some interesting facts about | the coins | . First | , there will be | one presidential US $1 coin | for each president | , except Grover Cleveland |. He will have two! Cleveland is the only U.S. president to have served two nonconsecutive terms. The last president now scheduled to get a coin is Gerald Ford. That's because a president cannot appear on a coin when he is still alive. In addition, a president must have been deceased for two years before he can be on a coin.

There are some interesting facts about the coins. First, there will be one presidential US $1 coin for each president, except Grover Cleveland. He | will have two | ! Cleveland | is the only U.S. president | to have served | two nonconsecutive terms |. The last president | now scheduled to get | a coin | is Gerald Ford |. That's because a president cannot appear on a coin when he is still alive. In addition, a president must have been deceased for two years before he can be on a coin.

There are some interesting facts about the coins. First, there will be one presidential US $1 coin for each president, except Grover Cleveland. He will have two! Cleveland is the only U.S. president to have served two nonconsecutive terms. The last president now scheduled to get a coin is Gerald Ford. That's because a president cannot appear on a coin when he is still alive . In addition , a president must have been deceased for two years before he can be on a coin .

依據文意，請判斷對錯。若是對的就在括弧內打 O，錯就打 X。
不確定是否正確時，請勿回答或猜測答案
（未回答的題目請計算為錯誤題數）

❶ （　　）

The Mint issues US$1 coins in order to honor former U.S. presidents.

❷ （　　）

A president can appear on a coin when he is still alive.

❸ （　　）

A U.S. president has his coin made two years after his presidential term is over.

❹ （　　）

On the heads side of the new US $1 coin, you can find the name of
a U.S. president.

❺ （　　）

President Grover Cleveland will have two presidential US $1 coins.

只花了 60 秒閱讀這篇文章，你答對了幾題？請對答案！
你的理解力 =(正確題數) 除以 5 再乘以 100% = ＿＿＿＿%

練習❻

〈單字〉

❶ puzzle

使（誰）感到困惑 (v.)

【例句】 That was a question that puzzled scientists.

❷ paradox

自相矛盾 (n.)

【例句】 That so many poor people live in this rich town is a paradox .

❸ emigrate

移民到某地 (v.)

【例句】 His parents emigrated to Canada last year.

❹ tight-knit

關係緊密的 (adj.)

【例句】 She hopes to have a tight-knit family.

❺ determinant

決定因素 (n.)

【例句】 Educational level was a major determinant of income.

請先花 5 秒鐘看看全文有多長即可 ⇨

練習❻

　　The Japanese have long puzzled public health researchers because they are such an apparent paradox: They have the world's lowest rates of heart disease and the largest number of people that live to or beyond 100 years despite the fact that most Japanese men smoke—and smoking counts as one of the strongest risk factors for heart disease. So what's protecting Japanese men?

　　Two professors at the University of California at Berkeley hoped to find out the answer. They investigated a pool of 12,000 Japanese men equally divided into three groups: One group had lived in Japan for all their lives, and the other two groups had emigrated to Hawaii or Northern California. It was found that the rate of heart disease among Japanese men increased five times in California and about half of that for those in Hawaii.

　　The differences could not be explained by any of the usual risk factors for heart disease, such as smoking, high blood pressure, or cholesterol counts. The change in diet, from sushi to hamburgers and fries, was also not related to the rise in heart disease. However, the kind of society they had created for themselves in their new home country was. The most traditional group of Japanese Americans, who maintained tight-knit and mutually supportive social groups, had a heart-attack rate as low as their fellow Japanese back home. But those who had adopted the more isolated Western lifestyle increased their heart-attack incidence by three to five times.

　　The study shows that the need to bond with a social group is so fundamental to humans that it remains the key determinant of whether we stay healthy or get ill, even whether we live or die. We need to feel part of something bigger to thrive. We need to belong, not online, but in the real world of hugs, handshakes, and pats on the back.

（103 年指考）

現在開始提升你的理解力吧！倒數計時 60 秒開始！

（第一段）

The Japanese｜have long puzzled｜public health researchers｜because｜they｜are such an apparent paradox｜: They have the world's lowest rates of heart disease and the largest number of people that live to or beyond 100 years despite the fact that most Japanese men smoke—and smoking counts as one of the strongest risk factors for heart disease. So what's protecting Japanese men?

The Japanese have long puzzled public health researchers because they are such an apparent paradox:｜They｜have｜the world's lowest rates of｜heart disease｜and｜the largest number of people｜that live｜to or beyond 100 years｜despite the fact that｜most Japanese men｜smoke｜—and smoking counts as one of the strongest risk factors for heart disease. So what's protecting Japanese men?

The Japanese have long puzzled public health researchers because they are such an apparent paradox: They have the world's lowest rates of heart disease and the largest number of people that live to or beyond 100 years despite the fact that most Japanese men smoke—｜and｜smoking｜counts｜as one of the｜strongest risk factors｜for heart disease｜.｜So｜what's protecting｜Japanese｜men？｜

（第二段）

Two professors │ at the University of California at Berkeley │ hoped to find out │ the answer . They │ investigated │ a pool of 12,000 Japanese men │ equally divided into │ three groups : One group │ had lived │ in Japan │ for all their lives , and │ the other two groups │ had emigrated to │ Hawaii or Northern California . It was found that the rate of heart disease among Japanese men increased five times in California and about half of that for those in Hawaii.

⇩

Two professors at the University of California at Berkeley hoped to find out the answer. They investigated a pool of 12,000 Japanese men equally divided into three groups: One group had lived in Japan for all their lives, and the other two groups had emigrated to Hawaii or Northern California. It was found that the rate of heart disease among Japanese men increased five times in California and about half of that for those in Hawaii.

（第三段）

The differences │ could not be explained by │ any of the usual risk factors for heart disease , such as │ smoking , high blood pressure , or cholesterol counts . The change in diet , from sushi to hamburgers and fries , was also not related to │ the rise in heart disease . However, the kind of society they had created for themselves in their new home country was. The most traditional group of Japanese Americans, who maintained tight-knit and mutually supportive social groups, had a heart-attack rate as low as their fellow Japanese back home. But those who had adopted the more isolated Western lifestyle increased their heart-attack incidence by three to five times.

The differences could not be explained by any of the usual risk factors for heart disease, such as smoking, high blood pressure, or cholesterol counts. The change in diet, from sushi to hamburgers and fries, was also not related to the rise in heart disease. However, the kind of society they had created for themselves in their new home country was. The most traditional group of Japanese Americans, who maintained tight-knit and mutually supportive social groups, had a heart-attack rate as low as their fellow Japanese back home. But those who had adopted the more isolated Western lifestyle increased their heart-attack incidence by three to five times.

The differences could not be explained by any of the usual risk factors for heart disease, such as smoking, high blood pressure, or cholesterol counts. The change in diet, from sushi to hamburgers and fries, was also not related to the rise in heart disease. However, the kind of society they had created for themselves in their new home country was. The most traditional group of Japanese Americans, who maintained tight-knit and mutually supportive social groups, had a heart-attack rate as low as their fellow Japanese back home. But those who had adopted the more isolated Western lifestyle increased their heart-attack incidence by three to five times.

（第四段）

The study shows that | the need | to bond with | a social group | is so fundamental | to humans | that it | remains the key determinant of | whether we | stay healthy | or | get ill, even whether we | live or die. We need to feel part of something bigger to thrive. We need to belong, not online, but in the real world of hugs, handshakes, and pats on the back.

⇩

The study shows that the need to bond with a social group is so fundamental to humans that it remains the key determinant of whether we stay healthy or get ill, even whether we live or die. We | need to feel | part of something bigger | to thrive. We | need to belong, not online, but | in the real world of | hugs, handshakes, and pats on the back.

依據文意，請判斷對錯。若是對的就在括弧內打 O，錯就打 X。

不確定是否正確時，請勿回答或猜測答案

（未回答的題目請計算為錯誤題數）

❶ (　　)

Most Japanese men smoke.

❷ (　　)

Smoking is a risk factor for heart disease.

❸ (　　)

In this study, those who often ate hamburgers and fries were more likely to suffer from heart disease.

❹ (　　)

Two professors at Berkeley found that the rate of heart disease among Japanese men decreased in California.

❺ (　　)

We need to feel part of a social group to stay healthy.

只花了 60 秒閱讀這篇文章，你答對了幾題？請對答案！

你的理解力＝(正確題數) 除以 5 再乘以 100%＝ _____ %

練習❼

〈單字〉

❶ column

　　雜誌或報紙的專欄 (n.)

　　【例句】Mike writes a weekly column for the New York Times.

❷ wheel

　　划著輪椅 (v.)

　　【例句】He sat in a wheelchair and wheeled himself into the elevator.

❸ rehearsal

　　排練 (n.)

　　【例句】She has a rehearsal on Friday.

❹ shooting

　　槍擊事件 (n.)

　　【例句】The shooting victim has stayed in the hospital for a week.

❺ paralyzed

　　癱瘓的 (adj.)

　　【例句】The car accident last year left him paralyzed.

請先花 5 秒鐘看看全文有多長即可 ⇨

練習❼

Wesla Whitfield, a famous jazz singer, has a unique style and life story, so I decided to see one of her performances and interview her for my column.

I went to a nightclub in New York and watched the stage lights go up. After the band played an introduction, Wesla Whitfield wheeled herself onstage in a wheelchair. As she sang, Whitfield's voice was so powerful and soulful that everyone in the room forgot the wheelchair was even there.

At 57, Whitfield is small and pretty, witty and humble, persistent and philosophical. Raised in California, Whitfield began performing in public at age 18, when she took a job as a singing waitress at a pizza parlor. After studying classical music in college, she moved to San Francisco and went on to sing with the San Francisco Opera Chorus.

Walking home from rehearsal at age 29, she was caught in the midst of a random shooting that left her paralyzed from the waist down. I asked how she dealt with the realization that she'd never walk again, and she confessed that initially she didn't want to face it. After a year of depression she tried to kill herself. She was then admitted to a hospital for treatment, where she was able to recover.

Whitfield said she came to understand that the only thing she had lost in this misfortunate event was the ability to walk. She still possessed her most valuable asset—her mind. Pointing to her head, she said, "Everything important is in here. The only real disability in life is losing your mind." When I asked if she was angry about what she had lost, she admitted to being frustrated occasionally, "especially when everybody's dancing, because I love to dance. But when that happens I just remove myself so I can focus instead on what I can do."

（101 年學測）

現在開始提升你的理解力吧！倒數計時 60 秒開始！

（第一段）

Wesla Whitfield, a famous jazz singer , has a unique style and life story ,
so I decided to see one of her performances and interview her for my column.

Wesla Whitfield, a famous jazz singer, has a unique style and life story,
so I decided to see one of her performances and interview her for
my column .

（第二段）

I went to a nightclub in New York and watched the stage lights
go up . After the band played an introduction , Wesla Whitfield wheeled
herself onstage in a wheelchair . As she sang, Whitfield's voice was so
powerful and soulful that everyone in the room forgot the wheelchair was even
there.

I went to a nightclub in New York and watched the stage lights go up. After
the band played an introduction, Wesla Whitfield wheeled herself onstage in a
wheelchair. As she sang , Whitfield's voice was so powerful and soulful that
everyone in the room forgot the wheelchair was even there .

（第三段）

At 57, Whitfield is small and pretty, witty and humble, persistent and philosophical. Raised in California, Whitfield began performing in public at age 18, when she took a job as a singing waitress at a pizza parlor. After studying classical music in college, she moved to San Francisco and went on to sing with the San Francisco Opera Chorus.

At 57, Whitfield is small and pretty, witty and humble, persistent and philosophical. Raised in California, Whitfield began performing in public at age 18, when she took a job as a singing waitress at a pizza parlor. After studying classical music in college, she moved to San Francisco and went on to sing with the San Francisco Opera Chorus.

（第四段）

Walking home from rehearsal at age 29, she was caught in the midst of a random shooting that left her paralyzed from the waist down. I asked how she dealt with the realization that she'd never walk again, and she confessed that initially she didn't want to face it. After a year of depression she tried to kill herself. She was then admitted to a hospital for treatment, where she was able to recover.

Walking home from rehearsal at age 29, she was caught in the midst of a random shooting that left her paralyzed from the waist down. I asked how she dealt with the realization that she'd never walk again, and she confessed that initially she didn't want to face it. After a year of depression she tried to kill herself. She was then admitted to a hospital for treatment, where she was able to recover.

（第五段）

Whitfield said she came to understand that the only thing she had lost in this misfortunate event was the ability to walk. She still possessed her most valuable asset—her mind. Pointing to her head, she said, "Everything important is in here. The only real disability in life is losing your mind." When I asked if she was angry about what she had lost, she admitted to being frustrated occasionally, "especially when everybody's dancing, because I love to dance. But when that happens I just remove myself so I can focus instead on what I can do."

Whitfield said she came to understand that the only thing she had lost in this misfortunate event was the ability to walk. She still possessed her most valuable asset—her mind. Pointing to her head, she said, "Everything important is in here. The only real disability in life is losing your mind." When I asked if she was angry about what she had lost, she admitted to being frustrated occasionally, "especially when everybody's dancing, because I love to dance. But when that happens I just remove myself so I can focus instead on what I can do."

Whitfield said she came to understand that the only thing she had lost in this misfortunate event was the ability to walk. She still possessed her most valuable asset—her mind. Pointing to her head, she said, "Everything important is in here. The only real disability in life is losing your mind." When I asked if she was angry about what she had lost, she admitted to being frustrated occasionally, "especially when everybody's dancing, because I love to dance. But when that happens I just remove myself so I can focus instead on what I can do."

> 依據文意，請判斷對錯。若是對的就在括弧內打 O，錯就打 X。
>
> 不確定是否正確時，請勿回答或猜測答案
>
> （未回答的題目請計算為錯誤題數）

❶ (　　)

Wesla Whitfield's physical disability was caused by a traffic accident.

❷ (　　)

Wesla Whitfield's physical disability happened when she was a college student.

❸ (　　)

Wesla Whitfield is paralyzed from the waist down.

❹ (　　)

Wesla Whitfield once suffered from depression.

❺ (　　)

Wesla Whitfield believes that the real disability in life is losing the ability to walk.

> 只花了 60 秒閱讀這篇文章，你答對了幾題？請對答案！
>
> 你的理解力 =（正確題數）除以 5 再乘以 100% = ＿＿＿ %

練習❽

〈單字〉

❶ long-span

長距離的 (adj.)

【例句】 He has seen many $\boxed{\text{long-span}}$ bridges.

❷ suspension bridge

吊橋 (n.)

【例句】 She likes $\boxed{\text{suspension bridges}}$.

❸ traffic artery

交通幹道 (n.)

【例句】 There are several $\boxed{\text{traffic arteries}}$ into the city.

❹ radical

激進的 (a.)

【例句】 He is a $\boxed{\text{radical}}$ politician.

❺ liberal

自由主義者 (n.)

【例句】 She is a $\boxed{\text{liberal}}$ in pursuit of political freedom.

請先花 5 秒鐘看看全文有多長即可 ⇨

練習 8

Opened in 1883, the Brooklyn Bridge was the first long-span suspension bridge to carry motor traffic, and it quickly became the model for the great suspension bridges of the following century. Spanning New York's East River, it provided the first traffic artery between Manhattan Island and Brooklyn. Before that, the only transportation was by ferries, which were slow and could be dangerous in winter.

The construction of a bridge over the East River had been discussed since the early 19th century, but the outbreak of the Civil War in 1861 deflected all consideration of the project. When the war ended in 1865, the bridge became an important issue once more. In 1867, the New York State legislature passed an act incorporating the New York Bridge Company for the purpose of constructing and maintaining a bridge between Manhattan Island and Brooklyn.

John Augustus Roebling was chosen to design the bridge. Born in Germany in 1806, he held radical views as a student and was listed by the German police as a dangerous liberal. He emigrated to America in 1830 to escape political discrimination.

Roebling proposed a bridge with a span of 1,500 feet (465 m), with two masonry towers in the East River serving as the main piers. The bridge that was actually built is longer—1,597 feet (486 m), the longest suspension bridge at that time.

（103 年指考）

現在開始提升你的理解力吧！請翻到次頁，倒數計時 60 秒開始！

（第一段）

Opened in 1883, the Brooklyn Bridge was the first long-span suspension bridge to carry motor traffic, and it quickly became the model for the great suspension bridges of the following century. Spanning New York's East River, it provided the first traffic artery between Manhattan Island and Brooklyn. Before that, the only transportation was by ferries, which were slow and could be dangerous in winter.

Opened in 1883, the Brooklyn Bridge was the first long-span suspension bridge to carry motor traffic, and it quickly became the model for the great suspension bridges of the following century. Spanning New York's East River, it provided the first traffic artery between Manhattan Island and Brooklyn. Before that, the only transportation was by ferries, which were slow and could be dangerous in winter.

（第二段）

The construction of a bridge over the East River had been discussed since the early 19th century, but the outbreak of the Civil War in 1861 deflected all consideration of the project. When the war ended in 1865, the bridge became an important issue once more. In 1867, the New York State legislature passed an act incorporating the New York Bridge Company for the purpose of constructing and maintaining a bridge between Manhattan Island and Brooklyn.

The construction of a bridge over the East River had been discussed since the early 19th century, but the outbreak of the Civil War in 1861 deflected all consideration of the project. When the war ended in 1865, the bridge became an important issue once more. In 1867 , the New York State legislature passed an act incorporating the New York Bridge Company for the purpose of constructing and maintaining a bridge between Manhattan Island and Brooklyn.

（第三段）

John Augustus Roebling was chosen to design the bridge. Born in Germany in 1806, he held radical views as a student and was listed by the German police as a dangerous liberal. He emigrated to America in 1830 to escape political discrimination.

（第四段）

Roebling proposed a bridge with a span of 1,500 feet (465 m), with two masonry towers in the East River serving as the main piers. The bridge that was actually built is longer—1,597 feet (486 m), the longest suspension bridge at that time.

依據文意，請判斷對錯。若是對的就在括弧內打 O，錯就打 X。

不確定是否正確時，請勿回答或猜測答案

（未回答的題目請計算為錯誤題數）

❶ （　　）

The purpose of building the Brooklyn Bridge was to replace an old bridge.

❷ （　　）

The Brooklyn Bridge is shorter than Roebling originally proposed.

❸ （　　）

The Brooklyn Bridge could be dangerous in winter.

❹ （　　）

John Augustus Roebling participated in the Civil War.

❺ （　　）

John Augustus Roebling moved to America in order to escape political
discrimination.

只花了 60 秒閱讀這篇文章，你答對了幾題？請對答案！

你的理解力＝(正確題數) 除以 5 再乘以 100% ＝ ＿＿＿ %

練習❾

〈單字〉

❶ anorexia nervosa

厭食症 (n.)

【例句】Some young women suffer from anorexia nervosa .

❷ realize

了解到 (v.)

【例句】They do realize the importance of education.

❸ subconscious

潛意識的 (adj.)

【例句】Some of our memories exist at the subconscious level.

❹ sorrow

悲傷 (n.)

【例句】 They felt sorrow at the death of Superman.

❺ consume

深深地影響 (v.)

【例句】 He was so angry and his anger consumed him.

❻ alter

改變 (v.)

【例句】 You need to alter your lifestyle.

請先花 5 秒鐘看看全文有多長即可

練習❾

During my ninth-grade year, I suffered from anorexia nervosa. It was not enough to be thin. I had to be the thinnest. Now, however, fully recovered, I can reflect back and realize that my wishes were more complex than fitting into size five pants. Many of my subconscious emotions were related to my relationship with my father. As I was growing up, his work always came first. Sometimes I would not see him for up to two weeks. Not only did he devote his whole self to his work, but he expected me to do the same ("You cannot get anywhere unless you go to the best universities!"). Though, consciously, I never felt pressure to please him, I began dieting after the first time he told me I looked fat.

At the time, all I knew was that I had to be skinny—skinnier than anyone else. Every month my father went to Europe for a week or so and on the days he left, sorrow and emptiness consumed me: Daddy was leaving. Then, I turned to focus on a mysterious weakness—a helpless childlike emotion that came from starving. I liked to know that I needed to be taken care of; maybe Daddy would take care of me.

Now, two years later and thirty-eight pounds heavier, I have come to realize that I cannot alter my father's inability to express his feelings. Instead, I must accept myself. I know that I am a valuable person who strives to achieve and accomplish. But I cannot strive solely for others. By starving, I attempted to gain pride in myself by obtaining my father's approval or acknowledgment of my value as a person. But the primary approval must come from me, and I feel secure now that I can live with that knowledge safely locked in my mind.

（97 年指考）

現在開始提升你的理解力吧！倒數計時 60 秒開始！

（第一段）

During my ninth-grade year , I suffered from anorexia nervosa . It was not enough to be thin . I had to be the thinnest . Now , however , fully recovered , I can reflect back and realize that my wishes were more complex than fitting into size five pants . Many of my subconscious emotions were related to my relationship with my father. As I was growing up, his work always came first. Sometimes I would not see him for up to two weeks. Not only did he devote his whole self to his work, but he expected me to do the same ("You cannot get anywhere unless you go to the best universities!"). Though, consciously, I never felt pressure to please him, I began dieting after the first time he told me I looked fat.

During my ninth-grade year, I suffered from anorexia nervosa. It was not enough to be thin. I had to be the thinnest. Now, however, fully recovered, I can reflect back and realize that my wishes were more complex than fitting into size five pants. Many of my subconscious emotions were related to my relationship with my father . As I was growing up , his work always came first . Sometimes I would not see him for up to two weeks . Not only did he devote his whole self to his work, but he expected me to do the same ("You cannot get anywhere unless you go to the best universities!"). Though, consciously, I never felt pressure to please him, I began dieting after the first time he told me I looked fat.

During my ninth-grade year, I suffered from anorexia nervosa. It was not enough to be thin. I had to be the thinnest. Now, however, fully recovered, I can reflect back and realize that my wishes were more complex than fitting into size five pants. Many of my subconscious emotions were related to my relationship with my father. As I was growing up, his work always came first. Sometimes I would not see him for up to two weeks. Not only did he devote his whole self to his work, but he expected me to do the same (" You cannot get anywhere unless you go to the best universities !"). Though, consciously, I never felt pressure to please him, I began dieting after the first time he told me I looked fat.

（第二段）

At the time, all I knew was that I had to be skinny —skinnier than anyone else. Every month my father went to Europe for a week or so and on the days he left, sorrow and emptiness consumed me: Daddy was leaving. Then, I turned to focus on a mysterious weakness—a helpless childlike emotion that came from starving. I liked to know that I needed to be taken care of; maybe Daddy would take care of me.

At the time, all I knew was that I had to be skinny—skinnier than anyone else. Every month my father went to Europe for a week or so and on the days he left, sorrow and emptiness consumed me: Daddy was leaving. Then, I turned to focus on a mysterious weakness—a helpless childlike emotion that came from starving. I liked to know that I needed to be taken care of; maybe

Daddy would take care of me.

（第三段）

Now, two years later and thirty-eight pounds heavier, I have come to realize that I cannot alter my father's inability to express his feelings. Instead, I must accept myself. I know that I am a valuable person who strives to achieve and accomplish. But I cannot strive solely for others. By starving, I attempted to gain pride in myself by obtaining my father's approval or acknowledgment of my value as a person. But the primary approval must come from me, and I feel secure now that I can live with that knowledge safely locked in my mind.

⇩

Now, two years later and thirty-eight pounds heavier, I have come to realize that I cannot alter my father's inability to express his feelings. Instead, I must accept myself. I know that I am a valuable person who strives to achieve and accomplish. But I cannot strive solely for others. By starving, I attempted to gain pride in myself by obtaining my father's approval or acknowledgment of my value as a person. But the primary approval must come from me, and I feel secure now that I can live with that knowledge safely locked in my mind.

依據文意，請判斷對錯。若是對的就在括弧內打 O，錯就打 X。
不確定是否正確時，請勿回答或猜測答案
（未回答的題目請計算為錯誤題數）

❶ ( )

Anorexia nervosa is an inability to express one's feelings.

❷ ( )

The writer suffered from anorexia nervosa when she was 18 years old.

❸ ( )

The writer's father told the writer that she looked fat.

❹ ( )

The writer's father wanted the writer to go to the best universities.

❺ ( )

The writer has been feeling secure since childhood.

只花了 60 秒閱讀這篇文章，你答對了幾題？請對答案！
你的理解力＝(正確題數) 除以 5 再乘以 100% ＝ _____ %

練習❿

〈單字〉

❶ copyrighted

　　有版權的 (adj.)

　　【例句】This is a copyrighted song.

❷ ownership

　　所有權 (n.)

　　【例句】The ownership of the house is still undecided.

❸ unaware

　　沒有意識到的 (adj.)

　　【例句】He was unaware of the problem.

❹ scare tactic

　　嚇唬人的手段 (n.)

　　【例句】She used scare tactics to keep her child away from fire.

請先花 5 秒鐘看看全文有多長即可　⇨

練習⓾

Downloading music over the Internet is pretty common among high school and college students. However, when students download and share copyrighted music without permission, they are violating the law.

A survey of young people's music ownership has found that teenagers and college students have an average of more than 800 illegally copied songs each on their digital music players. Half of those surveyed share all the music on their hard drive, enabling others to copy hundreds of songs at any one time. Some students were found to have randomly linked their personal blogs to music sites, so as to allow free trial listening of copyrighted songs for blog visitors, or adopted some of the songs as the background music for their blogs. Such practices may be easy and free, but there are consequences.

Sandra Dowd, a student of Central Michigan University, was fined US$7,500 for downloading 501 files from LimeWire, a peer-to-peer file sharing program. Sandra claimed that she was unaware that her downloads were illegal until she was contacted by authorities. Similarly, Mike Lewinski paid US$4,000 to settle a lawsuit against him for copyright violation. Mike expressed shock and couldn't believe that this was happening to him. "I just wanted to save some money and I always thought the threat was just a scare tactic." "You know, everyone does it," added Mike.

The RIAA (Recording Industry Association of America), the organization that files lawsuits against illegal downloaders, states that suing students was by no means their first choice. Unfortunately, without the threat of consequences, students are just not changing their behavior. Education alone is not enough to stop the extraordinary growth of the illegal downloading practice.

（98 年指考）

現在開始提升你的理解力吧！倒數計時 60 秒開始！

（第一段）

Downloading music | over the Internet | is pretty common | among high school and college students | . However | , when students | download and share | copyrighted music | without permission | , they | are violating | the law | .

（第二段）

A survey of | young people's music ownership | has found that | teenagers and college students | have | an average of | more than 800 illegally copied songs | each on their digital music players | . Half of those surveyed | share | all the music | on their hard drive | , enabling | others | to copy | hundreds of songs | at any one time | . Some students were found to have randomly linked their personal blogs to music sites, so as to allow free trial listening of copyrighted songs for blog visitors, or adopted some of the songs as the background music for their blogs. Such practices may be easy and free, but there are consequences.

A survey of young people's music ownership has found that teenagers and college students have an average of more than 800 illegally copied songs each on their digital music players. Half of those surveyed share all the music on their hard drive, enabling others to copy hundreds of songs at any one time. Some students | were found | to have randomly linked | their personal blogs to music sites , so as to allow free trial listening of copyrighted songs for blog visitors , or adopted some of the songs as the background music for their blogs . Such practices may be easy and free , but there are consequences .

（第三段）

Sandra Dowd , a student of Central Michigan University , was fined US$7,500 for downloading 501 files from LimeWire , a peer-to-peer file sharing program . Sandra claimed that she was unaware that her downloads were illegal until she was contacted by authorities . Similarly, Mike Lewinski paid US$4,000 to settle a lawsuit against him for copyright violation. Mike expressed shock and couldn't believe that this was happening to him. "I just wanted to save some money and I always thought the threat was just a scare tactic." "You know, everyone does it," added Mike.

Sandra Dowd, a student of Central Michigan University, was fined US$7,500 for downloading 501 files from LimeWire, a peer-to-peer file sharing program. Sandra claimed that she was unaware that her downloads were illegal until she was contacted by authorities. Similarly , Mike Lewinski paid US$4,000 to settle a lawsuit against him for copyright violation . Mike expressed shock and couldn't believe that this was happening to him . "I just wanted to save some money and I always thought the threat was just a scare tactic ." "You know , everyone does it ," added Mike .

（第四段）

The RIAA (Recording Industry Association of America), the organization that files lawsuits against illegal downloaders, states that suing students was by no means their first choice. Unfortunately, without the threat of consequences, students are just not changing their behavior. Education alone is not enough to stop the extraordinary growth of the illegal downloading practice.

依據文意，請判斷對錯。若是對的就在括弧內打 O，錯就打 X。

不確定是否正確時，請勿回答或猜測答案

（未回答的題目請計算為錯誤題數）

❶ (　　　)

It is common for students to download copyrighted music because they don't think that they will be caught.

❷ (　　　)

Both Sandra and Mike paid for downloading music illegally.

❸ (　　　)

RIAA believes that education provides great help in protecting copyrights.

❹ (　　　)

Suing students was RIAA's first choice.

❺ (　　　)

An appropriate title for this passage is How to Get Free Music Online.

只花了 60 秒閱讀這篇文章，你答對了幾題？請對答案！

你的理解力 = (正確題數) 除以 5 再乘以 100% = ＿＿＿ %

解答

第四堂課隨堂測驗答案

❶　I　　am standing　　on a beach.

　　WHO　　**ACTION**　　**WHERE**

❷　Mike　　opened　　the door.

　　WHO　　**ACTION**　　**WHAT**

❸　They　　looked at　　the running dog.

　　WHO　　**ACTION**　　**WHAT**

❹　Annie and John　　live　　in New York.

　　WHO　　**ACTION**　　**WHERE**

❺　I　　told　　her　　the truth.

　　WHO　**ACTION**　**WHO**　　**WHAT**

❻ His close friend   wrote   this book   in Taiwan.

     WHO   ACTION   WHAT   WHERE

❼ Annie   played   basketball   yesterday,

  WHO   ACTION   WHAT   WHEN

❽ Bruce   swallowed   the ping pong ball   by mistake.

  WHO   ACTION   WHAT   HOW

❾ One silly monkey   is swinging   in the trees.

    WHAT   ACTION   WHERE

❿ My friend   was seized by   some of the crew.

   WHO   ACTION   WHO

⑪ At the club,   I   drank   some beer and   ate   chips.

    WHERE   **WHO**   **ACTION**   **WHAT**   **ACTION**   **WHAT**

⑫ They   attacked   the village   and   killed

  WHO   **ACTION**   **WHAT**   **ACTION**

    many people.

     WHO

⑬ These days,   many young people   use   Instagram.

    WHEN   **WHO**   **ACTION**   **WHAT**

⑭ Jenny   wanted to play   her new toy   in her room.

  WHO   **ACTION**   **WHAT**   **WHERE**

⑮ The big bear   is sleeping   inside its dark cave.

    WHAT   **ACTION**   **WHERE**

⑯   Last week,   the dairy cow   was dancing   in my dream.

       WHEN   WHAT   ACTION   WHERE

⑰   The fat bees   were buzzing   around the hive.

       WHAT   ACTION   WHERE

⑱   In the deep dark woods,   the fluffy bunny   is bouncing.

            WHERE   WHAT   ACTION

⑲   John   bought   a blue umbrella with a black handle.

    WHO   ACTION   WHAT

⑳   On the 7th of August,   Vivian's husband John

          WHEN   WHO

   was reading   a book   in an apartment in New York.

    ACTION   WHAT   WHERE

第五堂課答案

練習一

❶（ ○ ）　❷（ X ）　❸（ ○ ）　❹（ X ）　❺（ ○ ）

練習二

❶（ ○ ）　❷（ X ）　❸（ ○ ）　❹（ ○ ）　❺（ X ）

練習三

❶（ X ）　❷（ X ）　❸（ ○ ）　❹（ X ）　❺（ ○ ）

練習四

❶（ ○ ）　❷（ ○ ）　❸（ X ）　❹（ X ）　❺（ X ）

練習五

❶（ ○ ）　❷（ X ）　❸（ ○ ）　❹（ X ）　❺（ ○ ）

練習六

❶（Ｘ）　❷（○）　❸（Ｘ）　❹（○）　❺（Ｘ）

練習七

❶（○）　❷（○）　❸（Ｘ）　❹（Ｘ）　❺（Ｘ）

練習八

❶（○）　❷（○）　❸（Ｘ）　❹（○）　❺（Ｘ）

練習九

❶（○）　❷（Ｘ）　❸（Ｘ）　❹（○）　❺（○）

練習十

❶（○）　❷（○）　❸（Ｘ）　❹（○）　❺（○）

第六堂課答案

練習一

❶ (○)　　❷ (X)　　❸ (○)　　❹ (X)　　❺ (X)

練習二

❶ (○)　　❷ (X)　　❸ (○)　　❹ (○)　　❺ (X)

練習三

❶ (X)　　❷ (○)　　❸ (○)　　❹ (X)　　❺ (○)

練習四

❶ (X)　　❷ (○)　　❸ (○)　　❹ (X)　　❺ (X)

練習五

❶ (○)　　❷ (X)　　❸ (X)　　❹ (○)　　❺ (○)

練習六

❶ (○)　❷ (○)　❸ (X)　❹ (X)　❺ (○)

練習七

❶ (X)　❷ (X)　❸ (○)　❹ (○)　❺ (X)

練習八

❶ (X)　❷ (X)　❸ (X)　❹ (X)　❺ (○)

練習九

❶ (X)　❷ (X)　❸ (○)　❹ (○)　❺ (X)

練習十

❶ (○)　❷ (○)　❸ (X)　❹ (X)　❺ (X)

Linking English
6堂課學會英文速讀

2019年7月初版　　　　　　　　　　　　　　　定價：新臺幣320元
有著作權・翻印必究
Printed in Taiwan.

著　　　者	周	昱		翔
叢書主編	李			芃
校　　　對	廖	倚		萱
整體設計	江	宜		蔚
編輯主任	陳	逸		華

出　版　者	聯經出版事業股份有限公司	總編輯	胡	金	倫
地　　　址	新北市汐止區大同路一段369號1樓	總經理	陳	芝	宇
編輯部地址	新北市汐止區大同路一段369號1樓	社　長	羅	國	俊
叢書編輯電話	(02)86925588轉5317	發行人	林	載	爵
台北聯經書房	台北市新生南路三段94號				
電　　　話	(02)23620308				
台中分公司	台中市北區崇德路一段198號				
暨門市電話	(04)22312023				
台中電子信箱	e-mail：linking2@ms42.hinet.net				
郵政劃撥帳戶	第0100559-3號				
郵撥電話	(02)23620308				
印　刷　者	文聯彩色製版印刷有限公司				
總　經　銷	聯合發行股份有限公司				
發　行　所	新北市新店區寶橋路235巷6弄6號2樓				
電　　　話	(02)29178022				

行政院新聞局出版事業登記證局版臺業字第0130號

本書如有缺頁，破損，倒裝請寄回台北聯經書房更換。　　ISBN 978-957-08-5333-9 (平裝)
電子信箱：linking@udngroup.com

國家圖書館出版品預行編目資料

6堂課學會英文速讀/周昱翔著．初版．新北市．聯經．
2019年7月（民108年）．240面．17×23公分（Linking English）

ISBN 978-957-08-5333-9（平裝）

1.英語 2.讀本

805.18   108008411